Risk Management

By Leeann Betts

Most people think accountants are boring.
Carly Turnquist, forensic account, is about
To prove them wrong. Again.

(c) 2020

ISBN: 978-1-943688-64-7

Cover designer: Donna Schlachter

Published by PLS Bookworks, Denver, CO

Where Publishing Dreams Become Reality

Cover photo courtesy of DepositPhotos.com

Chapter 1

When the office phone rang, Carly glanced at the caller ID.

And groaned.

Amanda, from Well Dressed, the only boutique shop in Bear Cove, Maine, which offered designer dresses for the discerning shopper. At least, that's what the sign over the door read.

Should she answer? Or let it go to voice mail?

Truth be told, she'd ignored the previous dozen or so calls. And the three messages over the past week—each one more frantic and making less and less sense.

She sighed. Yes, several months ago, fresh off her last extra-curricular crime-solving spree, she'd promised to help Amanda, her on-again, off-again friend. At the time, the woman's problem was tenuous. Something about an order from Peru that didn't arrive. Or didn't come in as expected. Or —

She snatched up the receiver. "Hello, Amanda."

A hiccupping half-sob traveled the telephone wire to her ear. "Oh, Carly, I'm so glad you finally answered."

Carly leaned back in her chair and propped one foot on the corner of her desk. "Sorry. I've been busy. Finishing up with a client. Preparing for the next. What can I do for you?"

From this angle, she had a delicious view of her backyard. Of course, February in Maine was nothing to write home about. Snow. Heavy cloud cover. Wind. She sighed. Maybe she'd convince Mike to move them south for the winter. Being self-employed, they could work from anywhere, so long as they had Internet. Then again, six months without seeing her kids or grands seemed a poor trade for sunshine and no snow.

"Well, my problem—which you aren't taking seriously, by the way—hasn't gone away. I'm sure you were probably hoping it would vanish like Christmas canes in January."

"Not at all. I never said that."

A deep inhale and exhale. "I know you didn't. But really. This is super serious."

Ah, now Amanda had her attention. Using those magic words: super serious. Still, Amanda was a tad more personable than her predecessor, Susan Markham. Perhaps dress shops emitted some kind of ion that sent its employees down the loony-bin trail. Like mercury did to Mad Hatters of old.

Carly plopped her foot to the floor and sat upright. "I'm all ears. Tell me what's going on."

"Can we meet for coffee? I'll close the shop. Heaven knows it's slower than cold molasses running uphill in January."

"Um. Sure. The Dew Drop Inn? At eleven? That's twenty minutes." A respite from these four walls would be good. "If you get there before me, order me a *breve*."

"What in the world is that?"

"Cappuccino made with half-and-half. It's decadent."

"If I drank that, my hips would be as wide as—"

Carly silently completed the sentence. *As yours.* "Victoria knows what it is."

"Eighteen minutes."

The line went dead. Funny how a woman who usually talked hrr leg off didn't take the time or energy to say goodbye.

Working from her home office meant Carly's normal attire comprised sweats and a t-shirt. She usually topped the outfit with—or toed it—with fluffy slippers which Doc the cat loved to chase as she headed for the bedroom to change. He wove in and out between her legs, crouching in the next spot where she planned to set her foot. She swerved

6

like a drunken sailor down the hall. Once inside the room, she kicked off the booties. The elderly marmalade chased them down, captured one and clutched it to his belly, back feet scrabbling.

Carly chuckled. "Doc, you are a mighty hunter still."

She bent and scratched him behind the ears as she headed for the closet, earning her a clawless bat. He was a great mouser, but he was also gentle as a kitten in his interactions with his humans.

She pondered what hung before her: jeans? Or slacks? This might be a business meeting. What about her black wool skinny-leg pants? If Amanda was seriously considering hiring her for her forensic accounting skills, perhaps she should dress up.

Then again, she'd accepted contracts before just as easily—and far more comfortably—in her indigo rayon stretchies.

A classic long-sleeved blouse and a tweed jacket were as much stylishness as she needed today. Besides which, no matter what she wore, Miss Fashion Plate would turn up her nose. Probably suggest she purchase more trendy articles at—where else?—her shop.

Sixteen minutes after she hung up the phone and two minutes before eleven, she slipped into the seat across from Amanda. True to form, the woman appeared as though she stepped out of the pages of Cosmo or another fashion rag mag. While her outfit was impeccable, something was off. Pale cheeks, dark circles under her eyes, her hair not carefully tended as usual. Plus, they weren't at the empty table next to the large plate-glass window. No, this time, Amanda chose a booth in the corner near the kitchen.

Definitely not her friend's usual choice.

Carly pasted on a smile. "Ordered yet?"

"Yes. Victoria gave me the evil eye when I told her what you wanted."

The owner of the town's only diner bustled over and set cups of steaming java on the table. "Nice of you to join us." She pulled out her order pad. "Want something to go with that?"

Amanda shook her head. "I'm fine."

Carly studied the hand-chalked board over the counter before deciding not to provide her friend with more ammunition. "I'm good."

Victoria tapped her on the arm with the now-unneeded booklet. "Yes, you are. Hoping you'll remember that come Sunday. Church is still open, and we have a potluck this week. Come as a guest."

"Thanks. I'll keep it in mind."

"You been saying that for a few months or more."

She tossed a genuine smile to this woman with a heart as big as Texas. "And one day, you'll see me there again."

Victoria chuckled and headed toward a table of newcomers. Carly sat back in the booth, toying with her drink until it cooled enough not to burn the roof of her mouth. The businesswoman was a gem, for sure. And one day, she'd do as she said. Go back to her church.

Just not now.

As Victoria said, she was fine. Church was only for people in trouble, right? And she had so little free time.

Time to get this meeting going. As The Duke would say: we're burning daylight. She did an elbow plant despite Amanda's sideways glance. "So, what's going on? You look ghastly."

Amanda's mouth lifted in a half-smile. "You stole my line."

"*You* called *me*. *You* need *my* help. I can go home and not worry about my elbows on the table or that my shoes are last year's."

Now a full smile flashed across the woman's face. "Last decade's, more likely." She sipped her coffee, then set the mug down. "You've been busy."

"When we talked before Thanksgiving, I returned from Colorado the day before. Next came the holidays. A couple of clients I had to finish up in January. Sorry I wasn't available." She lifted her *breve*, testing the temperature with her lip before setting it down again. Still too hot. "You said something about Peru. And a jungle monster? But I don't understand what's going on. Or why you seem to think it's so critical. Or mysterious."

Amanda's shoulders dropped an inch, and her hands stopped fidgeting with her beverage. "I have contact with a designer in Peru who works with folks who craft the most exquisite jewelry. Necklaces, earrings, brooches, bracelets."

"I recall seeing the display in your shop window."

"In October, I called him and placed an order. He said he might have some new samples to show me. He told me the first week of November he shipped the pieces that day. But when I received it, the package was opened. Nothing missing, mind you. The next day, I saw footprints in the snow behind the shop. And I was pretty certain the store was broken into, but nothing was forced."

"Did he send the samples?"

"No. But the point is—"

"I'm sure there are any number of people who travel that alley. And perhaps you forgot to lock the door?"

The younger woman waved off Carly's suggestions. "But if you'd seen the footprints. . . "

"What made you think monster?"

"One human boot, one cloven hoof."

"Oh, come on. In the snow, you said? Could easily have been somebody cut through the alley, then a dog or cat stepped near the print. What kind of monster has two different—"

"Many cultures, including Peru, have legends about mismatched feet on ghosts and demons."

Carly snorted. "Sure, legends. Fairy tales. Folk lore. Not truth."

Amanda shook her head. "Mock me all you want." She sipped her coffee. "I called the delivery company and told them about the package. They checked their records."

"And?"

"They *said* it was like that when they received it."

"But you didn't believe them?"

"Well—"

"You accepted that they were telling the truth?"

The shop owner's shoulders slumped. "I guess so. I mean, I couldn't prove otherwise. They said they checked the contents to the manifest before taping it up again."

"And that's how it was when you received it?"

"Yes."

9

"Do you really believe there was a monster in your alley?"

"I guess not." Amanda glanced around the diner. "Sounds silly, doesn't it, when we talk about it in the daylight like this?"

"Most bumps in the night don't hold up under a spotlight or a microscope."

"Well, that was until last week."

Great. Second verse, same as the first, no doubt. "What happened next?"

"My contact mentioned his friend came through this time, and he included several pieces as samples. But when I asked about details, he was cagey."

Carly straightened. *Cagey* wasn't a word she expected ever to come out of Amanda's mouth. "Maybe he's trying to make sure he stays as the middleman between you and his friend."

Her friend exhaled. "He knows I'd never go around him and cut him out. We've had other dealings in the past with other suppliers, and we had no problem."

"Could the pieces be illegal?"

"No."

"Stolen?"

A shake of her head.

"Counterfeit?"

"Don't think so."

She was running out of ideas. "Antiquities?"

This time, Amanda nodded. "Rogelio sent two packages at the same time. When I received the first yesterday, it was tampered with in the same way as the previous one. Rogelio always packages the items the same way. Individually wrapped in bubble wrap. Then each type of piece in a separate box."

Carly smiled at the shop owner's impeccable Spanish accent when pronouncing her contact's name. A rarity in this small town, particularly after Maria left. "What was different?"

"Two kinds of packing tape on the outside. He always uses white with his company name on it. There was an additional layer of clear. And

10

inside the box, several were torn open then taped shut again."

"Anything missing this time?"

"The samples. I called Rogelio, and he said they were there when he shipped it. The second package contained some last-minute pieces from his local suppliers. I called the company again, and they said the package was intact when it left their warehouse."

"Do you know how many pieces were sent?"

"He said four."

"And you think the samples were taken while they were on your doorstep?"

"Right."

"And that triggered your call today?"

"Well, yesterday I tried to think what might have happened. Assuming I believed the delivery company."

"Maybe parcel pirates here in town?"

"Why not take the entire package?" Amanda sat back and crossed her arms over her chest. "No, they knew what they wanted. And they took only that."

"What did you do next?"

"I called Rogelio and told him what happened. He got very scared. When I asked, he wouldn't say anything except that he'd call the craftsman and get back to me."

Carly sipped deeply of the creamy concoction, wiping the milk mustache with her paper napkin. No point in fueling Amanda's fashion diva sense. Perfect. "And did he?"

"Yes. Last evening. Even more afraid. Said his supplier was dead. Murdered. His body tossed off the side of a mountain."

Amanda paused and took several gulps of her coffee, and Carly used the opportunity to sip her own again. But this time, the beverage soured in her stomach. Talk of murder had spoiled her perfect drink. "That's terrible."

"And that's not the end of it. I asked what these samples were, and he wouldn't talk about it. Said awful things could happen. He didn't want to get involved."

11

"In smuggling antiquities out of the country?"

Amanda's eyes widened. "It's a big deal to some people."

"But not to others, apparently." Carly reached across the table and touched the woman's hand. Icy cold. "You need my help how?"

"To figure out what's really going on. But now that we've talked, I don't see how you can help."

"I *am* a trained investigator, remember."

"Sure. Numbers and stuff. But you don't understand anything about this."

"I've helped the police solve more mysteries than you have sets of false eyelashes, girlfriend." She tapped the table. "Carry on."

"He wouldn't say anything else. Except that the devil would be very angry. And not any run-of-the-mill devil. *El Chullachaqui.*"

"*El* what?"

"*Chullachaqui.* A Peruvian jungle monster. Mythical, I'm sure. But he sure seemed to believe it was real."

+ + +

Carly studied her friend who sat still as a statue across the table from her. Which was very unusual. Like her predecessor, Amanda liked to see and be seen. The fact she'd picked up on Amanda's choice of seating was now confirmed by the woman's admission that something was up.

She needed to pay more attention. "But this *El Chiquita* thing is a myth, right?"

Amanda shrugged. "Rogelio believes it's real. There's a whole cult following in Peru that says they've seen evidence."

"Such as?"

"Footprints on trails in the jungle."

Carly snickered. "Sounds like Big Foot. Or Sasquatch, depending on what part of the country you're from."

"I thought so, too. He sent me an Internet link to an article about how this creature can even change its appearance. There was a story about two men who went into the forest. One guy disappears for a few minutes. There's a loud scream, then he comes running out of the forest."

"And he says he saw it?" This was getting more and more bizarre

12

by the minute. "That's your proof?"

"No. The two men leave, and the guy who ran out takes the lead. And about a hundred yards down the trail, he changes into this strange little gnome-like creature." Amanda leaned forward and gripped Carly's arm. "And get this. One foot was human, and the other was a goat's foot." She sat back. "That's where it gets its name. Odd Feet."

"And what about the real man?"

"Never seen again."

Carly peered at her friend. She looked and acted as though she believed this tale. To Carly, it sounded more like a fable to keep children from wandering into the forest alone and getting lost. "I saw a movie about a backward community of people, living in isolation. They had a story about not going into the woods because monsters would get them. And sure enough, when somebody escaped, they ended up murdered."

Amanda leaned forward, eyes wide. "Here, in America?"

"Yes."

"That means there's more than one of them."

"No. It was a fable constructed in the late 1800s to keep people in the town. The leaders were sworn to secrecy and would terrorize folks who tried to leave. Think Amish town in a Stephen King movie. But it got out of hand, and people died. Finally, somebody managed to escape, and learned the world had moved on without them. The monsters weren't real."

"Well, that's a movie. I assure you, Rogelio doesn't live in a book."

"Why does he think this creature—and I'm not admitting I believe in it—would be involved?"

Victoria stopped by to refill Amanda's cup before strolling off to another table, coffee carafe in hand.

Amanda sighed. "Because of the antiquities. This creature is very protective of items from Peruvian history. Rogelio thinks perhaps his supplier stumbled on a large cache in a temple or a cave. He was an avid spelunker, after all."

"Not somebody you'd expect to fall from a mountain." She

13

pondered a recent news story she'd read about Mount Everest and climbers who fell to their deaths. "Although sometimes familiarity can breed risk-taking."

"Will you help me?"

"I don't see how. Seems like your problem is with Customs. Or parcel pirates. Perhaps the Peruvian or US post offices."

"He didn't send it by postal mail. He used the South American equivalent of an international courier service. Which then transferred the package to PackageExpress to deliver to me."

"Well, that should help. Still, you don't know where or when the package was opened. Or why. Might be that the thief stole only the most valuable pieces, hoping nobody would notice."

"Rogelio thinks the items came from a newly discovered Quechuan temple."

Now this was an interesting tidbit. "Like Machu Picchu?"

"Only one that his friend located."

"If that's true, whatever he uncovered belongs to the Peruvian people. Technically speaking, you almost accepted stolen property."

"I didn't know it was. And I didn't receive it."

Carly shook her head. "Makes little difference to the law. Conspiracy to export antiquities carries a hefty prison sentence in most countries. I don't know about Peru, but I suspect they aren't about to overlook this. I hear the prisons in Peru don't have cable television or crunchy peanut butter there."

Amanda's brow pulled down. "What are you dithering on about?"

"Inmates here in the US sued the government because they didn't have HBO or the expensive brand of PB." She sighed. "And they won. But don't expect such lush treatment in South America. I hear the Hanoi Hilton is five-star compared to prisons south of our border."

"I'm not going to jail in Peru or anywhere else. But I am worried about Rogelio. He's been my supplier for a long time, and I care about him and his family. He has a sweet wife and two darling children. We connect on FaceLink at least once a month."

"Sorry, didn't realize this was so personal for you. I thought you were all business." Carly tossed her friend a half-smile. "I have five days before I start on my next project. How can I help?" She held up a hand. "And before you ask, no, I am not going to Peru. I'll work from this end."

"I've asked Rogelio to see if he can track the package from when he last saw it. He says there has been an increase in theft in his country, particularly from packages coming to the US. He will ask about video at each sorting facility, the airport the parcel flew out of, and anywhere that plane stopped along the way."

"Great. Get me the tracking number—" She paused when Amanda slid a piece of paper across the table. "You were certain I would help, weren't you?"

Her friend smiled. "Where murder and mystery are concerned, you're all in."

Carly picked up the information. "I'll check with the driver here. See if he noticed the packaging. Maybe he can figure out how to work back through the chain of delivery. If the tampering happened in Peru, Rogelio will have to follow through."

"And if the theft occurred in the US?"

"I'll see what I can do. No promises."

"I'm happy to pay for your time."

Sweeter words were never spoken. Too many times her extra-curricular investigations didn't generate a penny. In fact, most often, they cost her. Time. Money. Mike's peace of mind. Still, Amanda was a friend. Sort of. "Let's see what happens. Could be Rogelio will find out the theft took place there, in which case, there won't be anything for me to do."

Her friend set several bills on the table before standing. "Coffee's on me. I'll arrange a FaceLink meeting with him later today. What time is convenient for you? You can update us on what you learned."

Carly bit back a response. Which part of letting Rogelio take the lead and confirm the pieces disappeared in their country of origin didn't Amanda understand? Still, she was acquainted with their local driver. Had his cell number, in fact. A call or two wouldn't take more than a few minutes. And Mike wouldn't be home until dinner time. "Four?"

"Great. That's five his time. Gives everybody the rest of the day to work on this. And bring good news to the table."

The rest of the day? That wasn't what she had in mind. Then again, if she buckled down, this mystery—and Amanda—would be off her plate by that time.

Because one thing was already decided—no monster was killing antiquities smugglers. Not in Peru. And not here.

The notion was ludicrous.

Wasn't it?

+ + +

Escaping *la policia* is never easy. And especially not under these circumstances. Normal routes of travel were now eliminated. Usual contacts refused to answer their phones or the frantic knocking at their doors. Even tossing notes left on their windshields or tucked into their bicycle baskets.

Everybody was *nervosa*.

And with good reason. It wasn't every day that people woke to one of the biggest manhunts Peru had ever seen. Armed militia patrolling alleyways and checkpoints on all major roads in the country. Increased police presence in every train and bus station, the airports, even in Lima at the shipping yards, searching for stolen antiquities.

Citizens wandering around in a daze, asking who could have contrived such a villainous act, let alone carried it out. Governments at all levels scrambling to find answers, to give information, and to claim the glory for themselves.

Well, they could accomplish none of it. At least, not while they sought a mastermind criminal ring. For despite their accusations and thinly veiled insinuations, their determination to identify and arrest the multitudes of criminals behind this heinous act, a single man and his unknowing friend were the perpetrators.

So long as I keep that piece of information close to my chest, the recovery and return would belong to one person, and one person alone.

Me.

And I have no intention of failing.

Chapter 2

Carly turned up her walkway, slowing to deadhead a rose bush of a handful of rose hips. Her best bet right now was to maintain an arm's length view of this whole situation, at least until something concrete materialized.

When she pulled her keys from her pocket to unlock the door, a wave of dizziness overtook her, blurring her vision. She grasped the door frame to steady herself and drew several deep breaths until the sensation passed. What the—? Too much caffeine? Not enough water? Well, she'd rectify that the instant she got inside the house.

But the lock wouldn't turn, although the key went in easily enough. She extracted it, then stared. The backdoor key, for goodness' sake. How could she make such a mistake? That silver key didn't fit the front door. Which was—was what? She fumbled through the bundle. Mailbox. That was easy. The smaller silver one. And the small brass one was for the shed at the rear of the house. This one with the orange tab was Doc's key—to his pet door. Ah, here it was. The silver key with the green cover.

Green for go. Go for go home. Little brass key for the little brown shed. Silver like armor and mail for the mailbox.

She recited the rules she'd made up to keep the contents of the ring straight. How had she mixed that up? Was it part of the aging process? Normal changes in hormones? Or something more?

Inside, she hung the keys on the rack by the door and slipped off

17

her shoes. The couch sure appeared inviting, but first things first. A glass of water. Dehydration it must be. Even though she didn't feel thirsty.

After gulping down the cool beverage, she headed for her office. While she told Amanda she wouldn't spend time on this mystery until she had more information, a little research wouldn't hurt. She could check out websites about the Peruvian jungle monster. Chuckle at the unlikely stories sure to appear under that search. Check out other articles about missing internationally shipped packages in the news lately. See if she uncovered anything about this dead spelunker/antiquities smuggler, or headlines covering recently discovered lost temples.

Any and all of this was bound to be interesting. An effortless way to pass the afternoon until Mike returned from a meeting with a client around supper time.

At least, unless the lights around her eyes and the thrumming in the back of her head signaled the return of her headache. Seemed she'd had several in the past month or so. Something she'd not experienced recently—at least, not in her peri-menopausal days.

And if she didn't feel better soon, she'd succumb to the siren call of her sofa.

+ + +

Once in her office, however, Carly slipped into work mode as easily as her feet eased into her furry booties. With Doc curled up on her lap, she searched the Internet for articles about the jungle monster. Then she checked out the website Amanda used to connect to Rogelio. Imagine how clear the grands would beam in from Riverdale, a mere hour's drive. Or even from New York City, where Tom, Sarah, and Bradley called home.

She sighed. Working out of her house called for much self-discipline. She'd have Mike help later with the connection program, and together they could figure out how to call the kids.

But now—now she had a mystery to solve.

There were hundreds—thousands, even, articles about the Peruvian jungle monster. Wow, way more results than she could check in a lifetime. She tried narrowing the search by using its given name, *El*

Chullachaqui. That was better. Still thousands, but more manageable.

Two hours later, Carly raised her eyes from her computer screen when her tummy rumbled. Doc stood and stretched, arching his back like a Halloween cat. "Yes, Doc. I hear you. Time to get supper started."

She stood, clutching the edge of the desk as the room swam before her.

Not again.

As before, she closed her eyes and took deep breaths until the vertigo passed. Not dehydration this time. She'd finished the last of her thirty-two ounce insulated mug with a straw moments before.

No, if anything, her brain was drowning in liquids.

Another tummy rumble. Then a total flip of her stomach and its contents. She clamped a hand over her mouth and headed for the bathroom. No point creating a mess she'd have to clean up herself since Mike still wasn't home.

Just in time she reached the toilet, and puked for several minutes until all that came up was a clear, frothy liquid. Had she somehow caught the flu? Fatigue and headache for several weeks. Now dizziness, blurred vision, and nausea.

If she were ten years younger, she'd think she was pregnant.

She chuckled to herself. Ten years ago—even five years—the thought would have cheered her. Now, her heart raced and her stomach turned over again as the butterflies fought for airspace.

Still, since she wasn't completely into menopause, might not hurt to buy another of those pregnancy tests down at the Olsen's Pharmacy. The last time she bought a test there, Mrs. Olsen was such a dear. Keeping her secret quiet, not an easy thing in this small town. And commiserating with her when the result wasn't what either she or Mike wanted.

Carly exhaled. That seemed like a lifetime ago. Three—no, four years. How much happened in those intervening years. Susan. The ranch. Bradley. Mike's college reunion. Gloria. Their Wyoming adventure. Phew. Wore her out simply thinking about it.

Or maybe that wasn't the reason she was so weary all of a sudden.

Simply standing here shouldn't make her tired.

She washed her hands and splashed cool water on her face before heading down the hall to the kitchen. What to have for supper? Leftovers? She checked the fridge. Not enough. Apparently Mike got into the container of lasagna from last night's meal and left but a small a snack.

She opened the freezer and stared at its contents. Pizza would do. And if he was still hungry, he could finish the lasagna. Right now, she wasn't certain she could get down more than a bite or two of anything.

She glanced at the clock while she unwrapped the three meat pizza. Half-past two. She had time to make a quick—or not so quick—run to the pharmacy and the bakery before her four o'clock with Amanda. A test and a torte. Or maybe a test and a couple of slices of pie. Best to check with Mike first.

She returned to her office and dialed his number on her cell, but reached his voice mail. "Hi, Mike. Pizza for supper tonight. I'm running downtown for—for dessert. Should be back in half an hour or less. Then I have a quick meeting with—with a potential client. Call when you get this so I know what time you'll be home. Love you."

Yes, she really loved this man. And his children who she called her own. And her grands, who were really hers. No step-anything in this family. Even her children's spouses were not in-laws but in-loves: son-in-love and daughter-in-love.

She traded her slippers for tennis shoes, grabbed her keys and her purse, and headed out the door. Her legs felt like they weighed a hundred pounds each. Trekking the half mile to the main drag again wasn't an option. She unlocked her car and slid in, started the engine, and backed out while fastening her seatbelt.

Once on Main Street, she found an empty space in front of the pharmacy and parked. The bakery was one door down the street on the opposite side. She could make it that far.

Entering the old-fashioned store was always like stepping into an *Andy Griffiths* episode. A u-shaped counter ran down both sides and met at the far end where the actual dispensing took place. In the open area at the middle of the store, several shelves stood, stocked with items folks

20

could peruse on their own. The walls were crammed with nooks and crannies bulging with everyday, non-embarrassing wares such as bandages and other home remedies, baby wipes and diapers and creams, body powder and hand lotion, hair dye and razor blades, and the like.

Mrs. Olsen turned from organizing some pill bottles. "Hi, Carly. Haven't seen you in a dog's age. Need any help?"

"Don't think so. I'll let you know if I do."

The older woman nodded and returned to her sorting. Mrs. Olsen reminded her of the perfect poster child for Grandmother of the Year, with her white hair pulled back into a bun, and her granny glasses perched on the end of her nose. Even her fifties-era dress and apron were reminiscent of Aunt Bea.

Thankfully, Mrs. Olsen still kept the intimate items in a small display in the center of the store, and Carly selected the same brand test she'd purchased before. Once. Jutting out her chin and pushing her shoulders back, she headed for the cash register and placed her choice on the counter.

Mrs. Olsen turned and smiled. "How are you doing? Mike well? And those kids and grandkids of yours?"

The woman's rapid-fire questions made Carly's head spin as she struggled to untangle her tongue. But the older woman didn't wait for an answer.

Instead, she glanced at the package and clamped her lips tight and made a zipping motion with her fingers across her mouth. "I won't say a word. Just like last time." She peered at Carly. "You're looking a mite peeked. Are you feeling unwell?"

"Nothing serious, I'm sure."

The older woman eyed her up and down. "Think you might be with child? It's a bit late in life, isn't it?"

"Just ruling out possibilities."

"Makes sense. This doesn't require a doctor visit until you're sure one way or the other. But if it isn't a child, what other symptoms are you having?"

Carly lifted one shoulder and let it drop. "Headache. Nausea.

21

Fatigue."

"Could be the flu."

"Right. But I'm also having blurry vision. Vertigo. I threw up today. And maybe sometimes fever and chills."

Mrs. O. nodded. "Still could be flu. Nasty strain going around this year. But it usually comes with a cough and upper respiratory stuff. Any of that?"

"No." Carly placed a bill on the counter to pay for the test. "Thank you for your discretion. I'll let you know the outcome."

"Thank you. See you again soon."

Carly exited the store and leaned against the wall. Maybe going to the bakery wasn't a good idea. Nope. She'd told Mike she would have a treat for dessert. If she didn't bring home something, he'd wonder where she'd gone. And she wasn't quite ready for that conversation. Not until she had a chance to see what the test said.

She'd go to the bakery.

She pushed off from the wall, veering to where her car was parked, and tossed her package on the seat. No point broadcasting her business to the entire world. Or at least the entire town. Which is what would happen if anybody else in town spotted her toting a pregnancy test around.

She waited until a vehicle passed before trotting across the street. Arriving at the opposite curb out of breath, her knees trembled, and perspiration gathered on her brow. By the time she pulled open the door of the *Sweet Tooth Bakery*, the chill afternoon air had dried the sweat. She wished she'd thought to put on a heavier jacket.

When she stepped inside, the bell over the door tinkled, and she stopped to inhale the delicious smells of breads and cookies. Then the odors gathered in her stomach and although she knew they weren't solid, they threatened to come up. Mouth breathing, she dropped into a chair at one of the several tables for customers, thankful it was there to catch her.

The swinging doors at the end of the counter separating the service area from the kitchen swung open, and Clara strode through, bearing a tray of goodies. The petite owner of the bakery set the latest concoctions on the counter. "Hi, Carly. Nice to see you again. Hope you haven't been waiting long." She glanced up at the bell. "Didn't hear that, but I think sometimes my brain is so used to it, it blocks it out sometimes."

"No worries. I've only been here long enough to catch my breath."

Clara's brow pulled down. "Doesn't sound like you at all, moving fast enough to need to regain your air."

"It's not. I've been feeling a little run down lately."

"Well, you sit right there, and I'll bring your order to you. Know what you want? Coffee while you wait? I brewed a new pot of that Jamaican mocha you really like."

"No, I'm fine. Enough coffee for today. But I'll take half a dozen of those pecan tarts."

"Gotcha. And I understand about too much coffee. Makes me all chatty and hyper."

Carly chuckled. "Sounds like you all the time. How would I know the difference?"

Now that her stomach had settled down and her head stopped spinning, she was feeling chatty and hyper, too. At least, in her own introverted way.

Clara packed the tarts in a small white box, taping it shut, and placed it into a paper bag with the bakery logo printed on the sides. Then she disappeared behind the display cases for a moment before ringing up the purchase on the register. "I added two cinnamon buns and a small loaf of whole wheat bread."

"I don't need all that. I only brought ten dollars with me."

"Not a problem. Enjoy them on me. Your tarts are four dollars."

Carly stood and dug the bill from her pocket, placing it on the counter. "Thanks so much. We'll enjoy all of it."

"Say hi to that handsome hubby of yours and don't be a stranger." She placed her change on the counter, and when Carly reached to retrieve it, Clara touched her hand. "You're looking a little tired. Dark circles under your eyes. Are you taking care of yourself?"

Touched by the woman's concern, Carly blinked back tears. "Not quite feeling myself for a couple of weeks. Likely the flu."

"Maybe you should get checked out. Could be anemia. Easy to correct."

"Thanks, appreciate it."

"I'll be praying for you, Carly."

Clara's words were like a warm summer's breeze, banishing the chill.

Carly smiled. "Thank you."

The ride home seemed longer than the trip downtown had been, but finally, she was back inside her own house again. She set the bakery bag on the coffee table and opened the package containing the test. She read the instructions—twice. The first time, her eyes couldn't quite focus on the words, making it seem like they were written in another language.

Ten minutes later, she emerged from the bathroom, test stick in hand. She stared at the symbol, unsure whether to be happy or not.

The front door opened, and Mike strode through. Early for a change. "Sorry I couldn't call. Couldn't get a cell phone signal—" He froze in his tracks when he saw her. And saw what she held. "Really? Again?"

She nodded.

"Got a result?"

Another nod.

He closed the distance between them. "Am I going to like the answer or not?"

"Depends."

"On what?"

"Whether you want a baby or not."

Chapter 3

One thing Mike could say about being married to Carly: there was never a dull moment.

He studied her across their kitchen table where he had insisted she sit. Now.

A baby.

Few men his age came into a scene with their wife holding a pregnancy test at arm's length as though afraid it was contagious.

And while they weren't having a child, she still hadn't been forthcoming on why she thought she might.

Time to clear up this enormous question.

He cleared his throat softly, waiting for her to meet his gaze. "How was your day?"

She lifted one shoulder and let it drop. "Oh, you know. The usual."

He chuckled. "Since when did *the usual* include a preg test?"

"True. Okay, some usual, and some not-so-much."

"Why don't you start at the beginning? And I don't mean an autobiography. After I left the house today, you. . .this is where you fill in the blank."

She leaned back in her chair and pulled her sweater around her neck. "Amanda called." She filled him in on her activities and conversations, leaving his head spinning. "Hopefully, now you understand why the test. I wasn't feeling well. Figured buying a test was easier than

25

going to the doctor."

"So, this Peruvian jungle monster. Is that what you're researching now?"

"Yes. I am expecting Rogelio to tell us he has evidence the theft happened on his side of the border. Honestly, anything between Peru and US Customs is out of our hands. And I'd rather not get involved with Amanda any more than necessary."

He tilted his head. This was new. "Thought she was your friend."

"She is. Sometimes." Carly turned her chair to stare out the window on a dismal and chilly afternoon. "But she hasn't quite forgiven me for the whole Susan affair."

"Which wasn't your fault."

"No, but I'm the face she remembers. The one she blames."

"So, why even take her call?"

"I thought it would be easy to turn her down. But when she mentioned a mystery creature, and she talked about Rogelio and friend dying, and—" She smiled at him, brightening every dark corner of the kitchen that even the sun couldn't reach. "Well, you see how I couldn't turn her down."

"Yeah. You were hooked." Some things never changed. Her curiosity, for one. He sighed. "What's next?"

"I meet her this afternoon at four, and we'll go over what I've learned. I figured if I handed over my research, that will be the end. It's obvious this creature is a myth, like Big Foot, and there's nothing we can do."

"You won't let it consume you, though. Will you?" He peered at her. "Don't you have other things to do?"

"Not really. She caught me at a convenient time. Between projects."

The doorbell rang, and she stood. "I'll get it."

"Did you order something?" He followed her down the hall. "I didn't."

"Two mystery novels. Can't wait to start them."

She rounded the corner from the hallway into the living room but

26

didn't quite make the turn. Instead, she wobbled on one foot, the other raised to the side, as though unable to place it on the floor.

Mike caught up with her and gripped her arm. "Steady there." He wrapped an arm around her waist. "Sit over here. I'll answer the door."

She blew out two breaths that lifted her bangs, shaking her head. "I'm fine. I can do it. Just stood up too fast."

He released her arm but hovered nearby. Didn't need her taking a face-plant. But as soon as she finished with the delivery, he'd sit her down and talk about what else was going on that she wasn't telling him.

She gripped the knob with one hand, steadying herself with the other on the door jamb, her knuckles white. "Hi. Oh, you're not Victor."

"No, ma'am. My name is Nate."

"Is Victor sick? Or is it his day off? Although, for the life of me, I can't remember him ever taking a day off. Not even for vacation."

"He took a few days off."

"Oh, did he go somewhere nice?"

"Don't know. Personal days, I think." The driver held an electronic scanner toward her. "Sign there. With your fingernail, please."

She released her hold on the door jamb and signed, accepting the box with the big smile plastered across it. "Thank you." Her gaze froze on something out of Mike's sightline. "If you see Victor, tell him I asked after him."

"I will."

"Nice tatt. I've been considering getting one. For my husband. Maybe a heart on my shoulder? Can you recommend your artist?"

"He doesn't live around here. Good-day, ma'am."

Carly closed the door and turned to face him. "That was strange."

Mike led her toward the sofa. "Besides you saying you're thinking about getting a tattoo?"

"He had strange artwork on his hand."

"Lots of people have tatts. Nothing strange there."

"But most people are proud of their body art. When I pointed his out, he shoved his hand into his pocket. And he wouldn't say who did it. Didn't want to talk about it."

"Let's sit a minute."

She complied but toyed with the box in her hands.

"Carly, we need to talk."

She continued staring at the box, picking at a loose flap of tape.

He touched her arm. "Carly." When she didn't respond, he repeated her name louder. "Carly. Look at me."

She lifted her gaze, her eyes wet but vacant. "What?"

"I'm calling the doctor for an appointment. For tomorrow."

And then the old Carly was back. "Why? Simply because I noticed a tattoo?"

He shifted on the sofa to face her. "What was strange about it?"

"It was shaped like a boat, and underneath it said THE TRAWLERS."

"So, maybe he's in a fraternity."

"Or a gang. More likely a gang. I mean, what college would have a social group named after a fishing boat? Unless it was a maritime college. Even then, they consider their graduates professionals, so I doubt they'd encourage body art." She shivered. "No, there's something going on."

"Such as?"

"He wasn't Victor."

"And that's important because?"

"Although his grammar was text-book perfect, there was something off kilter with his diction."

Mike chuckled. "Surely you're not against companies hiring non-native-born Americans? Not to mention, I know people born in this country where English isn't their first language, so they carry a hint of an accent."

Carly leaned back on the sofa. "Sure. New Mexico has its own accent, as do our American Indian tribes. I noticed that when we stayed at the dude ranch a few years back."

"So, what is it?"

"Not sure. For certain. Once I picked up on it, I listened more closely."

Mike shook his head. "You take great pride in being able to place accents and dialects."

She tossed him a wry grin. "You wouldn't believe how many people asked me if I was from Canada when I first came to Bear Cove. It was like the Midwest was a foreign country to them."

"You've got to remember many folks here haven't been further than Bangor, and the majority have never been outside the state. Bear Cove *is* their world."

"Well, Nate's accent was definitely not American. Not Canadian. And not from across the big pond, either. *Mexicano? Latino?*" Her brow drew down, reminding him of waves rippling on the beach. "And it wasn't so much an accent as it was the cadence of his words."

"I suppose you'll tell me you've heard it before. Isn't this how these conversations usually go?"

She closed her eyes. "I think I have."

"Carly, Carly. You said that the number of people without East Coast accents in Bear Cove could be counted on one thumb. And that would be you. You haven't been out of town for several months, so where did you hear that accent or dialect or diction or whatever you want to call it?"

"I travel virtually. And so do you."

"Where? When? Other than on television."

Her brow pulled down. "What did you want to talk about?"

"Your appointment with Doctor Walsh tomorrow."

She sat back. "I don't have one. Do I?"

Her widened eyes and slack-faced expression communicated volumes. She didn't remember their earlier conversation. Something was definitely afoot. "What else has been going on that you haven't told me about?"

She sighed and shrank like a balloon with a leak. "You're right. I haven't been feeling top notch for a couple of weeks. No, more like several months. Tired all the time. Headaches that go away for a bit but come back. Muscle aches. Vertigo. At first, I thought maybe I was getting the flu, but it went nowhere. Then the last few days, nausea. Fever. I threw up earlier today. That's why I did the pregnancy test. Just in case. I'm not completely through into menopause yet."

29

He patted her hand. "Anything else?"

"Blurry vision. I forget things. Sometimes I seem to zone out." She held up a hand to stop his next question. "And no, I don't know how long. Usually a few minutes." A tear dripped down her cheek. "I thought maybe I was dehydrated, so I drank lots of water. All that did was make me go potty more often." She frowned up at him. "Am I losing my mind? Or am I dying?"

He pulled her close. "Neither of those is likely to happen soon. But let's make an appointment so we can get you checked out."

She nodded and pressed into his chest. He rested his chin on her head.

She'd given in way too easily about seeing the doctor.

Perhaps her mystery gene was wearing off on him.

Something was afoot.

And it had nothing to do with a monster or missing jewelry.

+ + +

This woman must live the most boring life imaginable. First that visit with the shopkeeper. Surfing the Internet for hours. Unfortunately, the lack of sound meant no information on what she researched. Then a shopping trip downtown. The pharmacy and the bakery. Diet pills and doughnuts, most likely.

Almost as bad as drinking diet soda and eating a chocolate bar. *Americanos.*

She wasn't a problem though. She knew nothing, not even that she was being followed. A child could do this job. Perhaps hiring a teenager would be more efficient. She had no clue what was going on right here in this tiny village.

And now the husband was on the scene. He didn't seem very dangerous, either.

Too bad the seasons were opposite in the *Estados Unidos.* In Peru, summer with its warm weather, gentle rains, and sunny skies was much more pleasant than this rain, drizzle, and fog. Packing warmer clothes would have been wise. Now, a trip to the superstore near the motel was necessary. Standing outside, listening, was more difficult because windows

30

and doors were locked down tight. Still, their paltry security was no problem. Gaining access to their homes wouldn't prove difficult.

Edging closer to the house to hear their conversation proved another straightforward task. They were so naïve. What was that? Something about a baby? And what did she hold in her hand? No. Surely, she was too old for such things.

Then again, the notion she might be pregnant warmed the heart. Wasn't there a story in the Bible—perhaps more than one—of an older woman being with child? Was she excited? Or worried? No matter.

If she didn't keep out of this business, she wouldn't live long enough to experience either state for very long.

Chapter 4

When Carly arrived at Amanda's at two minutes before their appointment, she commended herself again for her excellent negotiation skills: Mike waited at home under the condition that she'd walk, not drive, to the meeting. And that she'd fill him in completely when she arrived home.

A suggestion she normally would take affront with until he reminded her she didn't always tell him everything.

Apparently, that was about to change. At least, according to him.

Before she raised her hand to ring the doorbell, Amanda yanked open the front door of her seaside cottage on Harbor Street. "About time you got here."

Carly flipped open her cell phone. "Not quite four. Did I miss the memo?"

Amanda ushered her in and pointed to the kitchen. "Coffee's on. And what memo?"

"The one where you changed the time of the call?"

Her friend exhaled. "Sorry. Rogelio has been on since 3:30. And he's like a cat on a hot tin roof, checking over his shoulder. Jumping at every sound. Threatening to take his family and disappear." She leaned closer. "And that's not all. I would swear somebody was outside my kitchen while I connected on FaceLink."

"Did you look out?"

"Through the dining-room window. But there's too many shadows from the setting sun."

"Do you have motion sensor lighting?"

The woman chuckled. "I do. I didn't think of that. It didn't come on."

"Maybe a branch scratching the window. Or perhaps a bat flew past."

In the kitchen, Carly poured herself coffee and selected two homemade chocolate chip cookies from the nearby platter. Where Amanda found time or energy to bake, she'd never understand.

Unless she asked. In which case, the woman would lecture her on organizing efficiently to accomplish more. Well, if that meant baking, she didn't want to hear about it. The Sweet Tooth Bakery on Main Street depended on her to keep them in business.

She exited through the back door leading to Amanda's yard and stood on the stoop. Probably best that she convinced Mike to relax at home while she met with Amanda. Now it appeared she had two mysteries on her hands.

Sure enough, the light fixture detected her presence and illuminated the area. She stepped down and strolled across the grass to the kitchen window. Peering at the grass, she detected a footprint and several bent blades but wasn't certain. Perhaps the lawn mower blade snipped the grass the wrong way.

Carly turned back to the yard and paused a moment. If somebody was there earlier, they weren't now. She shrugged and returned to the house. Amanda's imagination was running wild. Much as her own might in the same situation.

She locked the door then slid into a chair beside the one in front of Amanda's laptop. Sure enough, an olive-skinned man with flat features and black hair peered back at her.

His eyes widened. "Who are you?"

English was not his mother tongue, but he was well spoken with a delightful accent a little different from other Hispanic speakers. Different than Nate's, but similar.

She smiled at him. Maybe he'd chill out if she appeared friendly and harmless. "I'm Carly, Amanda's friend."

34

"Ah, jes, she mention jou." He glanced around a couple of times. "Jou hear that?"

"No. What?"

"Noise outside." He turned. Rattled off some gibberish Carly knew was Spanish but didn't understand. "*Mi esposa.* Carmen."

His wife. Carly didn't speak *Espanol* and understood not much more, but that she got. Amanda wasn't exaggerating. This guy was super nervous. "How is the weather?"

"Huh?"

"Rain? Sunny? Cold? Warm?"

"Oh, si. Is summer end here. Our winter start in few month."

Thankfully, Amanda sat beside her and spoke a few sentences in Spanish to Rogelio. Carly didn't understand what she said, but at least the worried man settled in his chair, his shoulders relaxed and the creases gone from around his eyes and mouth.

Amanda turned to her. "He thinks somebody has been following him. Watching where he goes and who he meets. Conducting business has been difficult." She faced the screen again and asked a question, listened, then turned to Carly again. "They have a small house in a town about an hour's travel from their home where they can stay until he is certain the threat is over."

"How will he be certain when the threat is past? And does he even understand what this trouble is? Perhaps he's paranoid over his friend's death."

Amanda peered at her. "Not death. Murder. Somebody pushed his friend off a mountain ledge after they cut his tether rope. The police are investigating, although Rogelio has no confidence they'll identify the killer. Too many will agree his friend was wrong for trying to take the stuff out of the country and that he deserved punishment."

"Okay." There was a tiny gray area between paranoia and reality, and the old ditty came to mind: JUST BECAUSE YOU'RE PARANOID DOESN'T MEAN THEY AREN'T OUT TO GET YOU. "What will he do next?"

Amanda asked another couple of questions in Spanish then translated. "He checked at the local delivery office, saying some items

35

were missing from the order. They will provide him video from along their transit route. Their liaison will contact the air transport company and ask for video. His contact says if either of these parties opened the package, they'd include an official document and re-seal the box using logo-branded tape. Rogelio doesn't think they opened it there. At least, not legitimately."

Carly scooted forward in her chair. "An employee could have tampered with it, but not for business purposes?"

"Right. So, what are you going to do?"

"Well, like I told you, I only have five days before my next case starts." Carly pulled out her phone to confirm her calendar. "I'll wait and see what Rogelio might learn. We can meet first thing in the morning, then hopefully we'll have more information. I'll continue investigating from this end then."

Amanda grunted. "If that's the case, I'm glad you are getting to work on this right away."

Carly bit back her retort. Seemed she and Rogelio had the most work to do on this matter, while the person with the dog in the fight— Amanda—did nothing but arrange meetings. "I don't think—"

Amanda held up a hand to stop her while she translated her intentions back to Rogelio, although he nodded his understanding of most of what Carly said. "Sounds like a plan." She turned to the computer. "We'll meet again tomorrow morning at nine your time, eight ours. See what you learned and where we'll go from there. *Adios, and buenos dias.*"

The screen showing her Peruvian friend's face closed, and Amanda disconnected the call. "I sense hesitation on your part about this. I was hoping you'd get on this right away."

"No point in wasting valuable resources if he finds out the theft occurred before the package ever touched American soil. Neither you nor I have jurisdiction or contacts outside the US. Watch some relaxing television tonight and try to put this out of your mind for now."

Amanda harrumphed. "Sure. Like that's about to happen." She wrung her hands. "I cannot carry on as though nothing has happened. I feel violated."

"I understand. But—"

The shopkeeper held up her hand again. "If you understood, there would have been a period at the end of your first sentence."

There was no winning this battle. Carly sighed. "Fine. I'll see you tomorrow. No promises I'll have any more information than I do now, though."

Amanda smiled. "I trust you, Carly. My business is in your hands. You won't let me down."

Her friend's tone of voice communicated that her last words were more of a command than a statement of fact. "I'll do my best. Keep busy so you aren't fretting."

As Carly returned home, she questioned her own advice. Would she go on with her normal routine if this were happening to somebody she loved, such as her kids or grands? Amanda obviously cared for Rogelio and his family. Certainly, they enjoyed more than a casual business relationship. Could missing jewelry linked to a South American country call this businesswoman's ethics into question? Might suspicions of drug smuggling arise?

No, if she found herself in her friend's shoes—which she had in the past—she'd not step down until she had the answers to all the questions.

Problem was, did she have any idea what information she even needed?

As she rounded the corner to her street, she compiled a list in her head of the missing pieces of jewelry. Some idea of where they might be. And why. Unfortunately, neither Rogelio nor Amanda had that information.

Because if they did, why wouldn't they speak up and save everybody all this hassle? Unless one of them realized the historical and black-market value of the objects and wanted to cash in for themselves. She didn't know Rogelio at all. And what about Amanda? The woman was a fair-weather friend. Perhaps fair-weather *acquaintance* was a better description. Susan, Amanda's former employer and the previous owner of the shop, was more of a friend—and see how that turned out.

Who knew so much information could be gleaned by pressing an ear against a window? And when the homeowner looked out? Exciting! Held my breath. Froze in place. Just like in a spy novel.

And that other woman? The one with the pregnancy test. Better than *la policia*. With their flashlights and snarling dogs. And guns. Still, she'd seen something in the grass. Careless. As they say in the US: Note to self. Be more careful.

Exhale. Shake off the exhilaration. Time to go. Book into the motel up on the highway. Probably a flea box—no, that wasn't the term. Flea *bag*. Nothing five-star in this small town. No matter. The time here would be short and to the point. Find the other necklace. Eliminate whoever gets in the way. Get back to Peru. Return the artifact to its rightful place.

As these *Americanos* say, easy-peasey.

Chapter 5

The next morning, Carly dragged herself out of bed more tired than when she crawled under the covers the night before. The room swam before her eyes, so she sat on the edge of the mattress for a few minutes until gathering enough strength to stumble to the shower.

Emptying almost their entire fifty-gallon water heater enabled her to regain her sense of humanity again. She toweled off, combed her hair, then headed for the kitchen. Coffee and bacon smells wafted toward her. Mike was already up and making breakfast.

But as soon as she stepped through the doorway of the dining room into her favorite room, her stomach lurched. She pulled out a chair and planted her butt firmly before her legs gave out beneath her. Mike, whistling his endless song and busy at the stove, didn't turn around, so she took several deep breaths.

Come on, body. Smarten up. You're too young for this kind of shenanigans. Whatever kind it is.

Finally able to turn her head without falling off the edge of the world, she pasted on a smile. If she didn't want to arouse his suspicions that something serious was affecting her health, she needed to press forward. Stiff upper lip, as the British said.

"Good morning, Mike."

He turned to face her, a whistle trapped behind his teeth. "Hi, gorgeous. Coffee?"

"That sounds good."

"How'd you sleep?"

"Like a log."

Which was true. And an apt description for how she still felt. But wild horses wouldn't drag that confession from her.

He placed her mug on the table, already doctored with cream and a touch of sugar. "Food will be three minutes. Wrap your hands around that and warm them up."

She clutched her hands into fists. They were chilly. "How did you know?"

His brow furrowed. "Just an expression." He set the spatula down and reached across the table, placing his warm ham-sized hand on hers. "But you're right. They are like ice cubes."

She extracted her hand and picked up her mug with both, not entirely certain one would do the job. Then she sipped, savoring the rich flavor. "Hmm, good. As always. You make the best coffee."

"Scrambled eggs, bacon, and hash browns okay?"

"Half portion of each, please."

This time his mouth turned down, too. "Tummy upset?"

Thankfully, not this morning. But she still didn't think she could get much down. She smiled. "The doctor will probably weigh me this morning, and I don't want to explain that I had a twenty-pound breakfast so he won't lecture me on getting more exercise and eating less junk food."

Mike chuckled and turned back to the stove. "Half portion it is. Don't worry about the exercise thing. He already knows your set number of heartbeat theory."

"I subscribe to that belief seriously. If we're given a certain number of heartbeats to last our entire life, why waste them on exercise?"

He spooned food onto two plates then sat at the head of the table to her left. "As always, anything you can't eat, push over onto my plate."

She glanced at the clock. Half past seven. "I'd best hurry. I said I'd meet with Amanda again this morning."

Mike forked in a mouthful of eggs, chewed and swallowed. "Thought you covered all that yesterday?"

"We didn't go over my research, and she wants us all on the same page, as she calls it."

"Don't let her push you around."

Carly managed half a forkful of eggs down then washed it all the way with coffee. "I won't. But you must admit this is an intriguing mystery."

Mike chewed on a strip of bacon, working his way from start to finish then licking his fingers before nodding. "Maybe. Or it might simply be overblown. I mean, this is how the media often gets it wrong. In their rush to report on a story, they expand conjecture and insinuations into fact and reality. Later on, when they learn more, they drop that first line of inquiry and latch onto something else. But folks don't forget the first article."

Carly cut her bacon into tiny pieces, speared one bit, pushing it up on the tines, snagging a mouthful of potatoes. "How does that apply in this case?"

"Well, according to what you told me, a witness says he saw an animal push Rogelio's friend over the cliff and cut his rope. The police say they see what they claim are this monster's footprints. Maybe the next report will mention somebody else saw mountain goats, which explains the mixed prints. But people only remember mention of the monster and believe it killed him."

"I guess that could happen."

"Could happen? No, it does, all the time. Think about that airplane that crashed a few months back. First reports said they saw some kind of missile flying toward it. But the FAA said the flames weren't from the tail of a drone, but from the engine not burning fuel properly, and it exploded and caused the plan to crash."

"Yeah, I remember that." She rubbed at the base of her neck where that pesky headache simply wouldn't leave. "Time to go. You coming with?"

"I don't want you out by yourself until we figure out what's going on with you. Sure. I'll come." He shoveled in the last few bites on his plate and on hers, gathered the dishes, and set them on the counter.

41

"Come on. I'll clean that up later. I'll drive to Amanda's, and after that we'll go to the doctor's. The appointment is at nine-thirty."

Great. Just what she looked forward to. Perking up her day by seeing Amanda again, then a doctor's visit.

Was it too late to go back to bed?

+ + +

Feeling like she led a short parade, Carly rang Amanda's doorbell at five to eight with Mike beside her. She clutched her folder of printouts—maybe fifty pages—in one hand while he gripped her other.

The sun struggled to poke through the dense cloud cover, leaving the town still clothed in the shadows of dawn, and fog rolled in from over the harbor. Usually she enjoyed mornings like this. Loved seeing streetlights that stood as beacons against the receding gloom. Enjoyed when the two-tone foghorn of the local lighthouse punctuated the silence.

But not today. Not with whispers of murder and criminal activity.

Not to mention her concerns about her health.

And the whole baby scare thing.

Amanda opened the door, her eyes widening when Mike stepped forward. "Hi, Mike. Wasn't expecting you."

"Came along to keep Carly company."

Amanda turned her attention to her. "Oh. You could have driven."

"Needed the exercise. You don't mind, do you?" She shivered. She wouldn't let Amanda's peevishness get her down. "He might offer insight into the problem. Maybe he knows other computer geek stuff we could do."

The younger woman stepped back, the hall light illuminating her. Tendrils of hair escaped a messy bun-thing gathered on the top of her head. Her pants wrinkled—and was that a coffee stain on her blouse? Not like Amanda to be anything less than perfectly outfitted and coordinated at any time of the day or night.

"Come in. Coffee's on."

Sounded great, but—. "Thanks. Already had my limit for the day. I'd better stick to water or decaf something."

42

Mike shuffled along close behind her, his grip on her elbow coming threateningly close to her funny bone. And, as everybody knew, there was nothing hilarious about setting off that particular nerve.

She glanced over her shoulder, keeping her voice low. "A little space, please?"

He nodded but kept hold of her.

Amanda led her into the kitchen as she'd done earlier in the day. Her laptop still sat on the table, but now what looked like a ream of papers was strewn across its surface.

Something was up. The shop owner was even more fastidious about paperwork and keeping it in order than she was. She quirked her eyebrows toward the mess. "Explosion in the paper factory?"

"I spent the evening going through past invoices and checking them against inventory and sales. Something is definitely wrong."

"What?" Carly slid into the chair she'd occupied earlier, and Mike sat across from her. "Do you think this has happened before?"

"No. It was something Rogelio said. He was emphatic his supplier had five pieces."

"Right. And you didn't get any of them." When Amanda set a glass of water before her, Carly nodded her thanks. "So, what was bugging you?"

The woman sat in her place in front of the laptop. "I wondered if Rogelio could be wrong. And that maybe it happened before."

"You think he's been shorting you on your orders? He seemed a nice enough guy."

"Oh, he is. I don't doubt him. I was wondering if my packages had been opened in the past and I didn't notice. So, I checked my invoices against my inventory."

"And?"

Amanda exhaled and slumped into her chair. "Nothing. Everything was spot on."

"Well that's marvelous news, right?"

"Guess so."

Mike sipped his water before setting the glass down. "It begs the

43

question of why somebody tampered with this order." When Amanda turned to him, he offered her a half-smile. "Carly filled me in on what's going on."

"That's just it. What *is* going on? I mean, why would some random thief target my package? Artisan jewelry from Peru shipped to a small store in Nowheresville, USA."

"Good question." Carly picked up several pieces of paper and scanned them. "So, everything is in order?"

"Seems to be."

Carly didn't like the conclusion she was about to speak, but saw no way out of it. "This wasn't random. It was targeted. And since it only happened when a new supplier included some mystery pieces, the reason must be linked to the items."

The computer pinged, and Amanda straightened. "Rogelio is on FaceLink." She clicked a button and pasted on a smile. "Hi, Rogelio. Hope you have something good for us." When Carly and Mike both scooted around the corner of the table, Amanda introduced them. "You remember Carly? She's helping with our investigation."

"*Sí*, hello again." His eyes darted from one side of the screen to the other. "And this man?"

"Carly's husband, Mike. He accompanied her today. I thought he might help us, too. He's a very intelligent man."

Carly gritted her teeth. Just like Amanda to make any good idea sound like her own.

Mike, however, nodded and smiled at the screen. "Hello, Rogelio. Nice to meet you."

"*Y tu.*"

Amanda pulled a notebook and pen closer. "Did you find anything?"

"*Sí.* Much additional information. But I don't think you will like what I have to say."

Carly's stomach sank to her toes.

Nothing good ever came from an opening like that.

And she doubted his would be any different.

Amanda picked up her pen. "Let's start with what Carly found first."

Then Amanda pointed to Carly's folder of printouts from her online research. "Want to share what you learned?"

"Probably nothing Rogelio doesn't already know."

She went through each news article and website printout, detailing the legend of the monster and its impact on local culture. While many tried, nobody had ever disproven the myth. In fact, its belief was widespread, extending beyond the Quechuan culture. Although other legends shared some similarities, there were also differences between this half goat-half man creature and others around the world.

Then she gathered the pages into a neat pile. "Anything else you'd like to add, Rogelio?"

"*Sí*. Not about the monster. I call PackageExpress office, and they tell me come and see video. They scan packages many times along route so customers can track. I see package scanned and placed in bin to go to airport. Then they show me where package arrived and scanned at airport. All good."

Amanda paused, her pen resting on the paper. "Is that all?"

He shook his head, his dark eyes serious. "Cannot see more video of arrival in Lima to transfer to plane that go to America. Nobody return my call. But I call US Customs, and they tell me if they opened, they put in document. And they use—uh, what the word? Packing tape that say US Customs, so that not who opened. Also, package weighed here in Cusco by PackageExpress, and Customs weigh also to make sure nothing added or removed en route. Same weight. So, didn't happen in Peru or Lima." He sat back and folded his arms over his chest. "Thief in US."

Mike leaned forward. "All sounds serious. Anything else?"

Rogelio held up a newspaper. "Nothing in today's paper about either the temple or my friend's fall. I think they hope people will forget." His shoulders sagged. "But I will not forget. I will call the police again in a few days. Maybe travel to Iquitos if they don't talk to me."

Carly leaned forward. "Might that be dangerous?"

"Why? I not criminal."

45

"No, but if the police and other officials want to keep this story quiet, they might see you as a threat. And if the killer learns you're looking into it, he might worry you will uncover clues. Which could lead to the belief it wasn't a mythological creature that killed your friend."

Rogelio's brow pulled down. "What is this myth—myth—logical? *El Chullachaqui* is real."

Amanda patted Carly's hand. "What she meant is we don't want to put you in danger."

"I already in danger. Somebody follow me. Break into my home." The Peruvian native's hands clenched. "Somebody steal paper."

Mike frowned. "What paper?"

"Bill of lading for package."

"Nothing else?"

He shook his head. "No."

Carly leaned forward. "Excellent work, Rogelio. I hadn't thought about checking with US Customs, or about the weight." She sat back and glanced at Amanda and Mike. "So, that puts it in our ballpark."

Rogelio chuckled. "You think you find in sports arena?"

Amanda shook her head. "It's a figure of speech here in the US. Means now it's up to us to find it."

"Ah." He turned to someone off-camera, spoke then turned back. "My wife, Carmen. She say I should tell what else I found out."

Amanda nodded. "We're ready."

"I call police in Iquitos where my friend die. They say he not the good man I thought. He brag about finding a lost Incan temple."

Amanda gasped. "That doesn't sound good."

"No. Nothing wrong with finding temple. Wrong if he didn't tell government. Cannot take items from temples and historic sites in our country."

Mike shifted in his seat. "It's the same here, too, Rogelio. We can't even take rocks or plants from our parks."

The Peruvian man's eyebrows raised, disappearing beneath the hair lying across his forehead. "Same here. Police in Iquitos investigate him when they learn of this. Go back to where he killed."

46

Now this was exciting news. A murder linked to an old temple. Felt very Pyramid-ish. "Did they find the temple?"

"Yes. One not known before. They send team of—oh, what is called?" He snapped his fingers a couple of times as though prompting his memory. "Scientists who open old tombs and find bodies. Who dig into ground?"

Ah, this one Carly knew. "Archeologists."

"Yes. They climb down into cavern and find temple. They find much treasure. Wall paintings of five priests wearing necklaces. Each piece different. But they no find necklaces."

Mike exhaled. "Sounds like your friend might have taken the necklaces, perhaps intending to go back and pillage the temple once Amanda agreed to buy from him." He turned to the businesswoman. "Why would he believe you could move high-end jewelry like that?"

She shrugged. "I mean, the most expensive pieces I sell top out at two hundred dollars."

Carly frowned. "Do you sell to more than folks from around here?"

Amanda straightened, pressing her shoulders back. "Yes. In fact, most of my sales are from online customers."

Huh? "Online customers?"

"Yes. Through my website. Discriminating buyers from all over the country—all over the world, actually—order from me."

Well, who would have thought such a thing was possible? Not that many folks would buy her forensic accounting skills that way. No, that was more credibility-based and word-of-mouth. "So, if this friend stole the items, could somebody else have known what he was doing?"

Rogelio nodded. "Witness say he was nearby the day my friend killed. Saw him at top of cliff. Saw animal come up from behind and push him over ledge. Then saw animal do something to rope. My friend fall to death."

Carly snorted. "Animals don't cut ropes. And they don't murder people."

Rogelio shrugged. "Is how witness saw it. Police investigate and

47

find tracks. One human, one goat." He stared at them across the miles. "*El Chullachaqui.*"

Mike edged in closer. "Does this sound like something your friend would do?"

A half-shrug. "Maybe. He always want way to get rich quick without work. And he no like government. If he saw way to keep something from government and make money, I think he do." His chin dropped to his chest. "But he no deserve to die."

Carly sat back. "You know what this means, don't you?"

Amanda turned to her. "What?"

"They—whoever they are—can track where the package was mailed. They have your address here in Bear Cove."

The words hung in the air, heavy and full of implication.

While Carly didn't agree that stealing cultural artifacts was right, she did agree it wasn't worth killing somebody for.

But it seemed others felt more passionately about their antiquities.

Enough to murder for.

+ + +

This news of the package's weight—a careless oversight. The items should have been recovered inside the country, but no, Rico was too stupid and inept to accomplish that simple task. Which precipitated this dangerous mission on foreign soil.

Thweph. Spit on Rico's mother's grave. Bette yet, spit on Rico's grave. His inability to follow simple orders would surely be noticed higher in the organization.

And dealt with accordingly.

As would anybody interfering with the successful conclusion of this assignment.

El Chullachaqui.

If that's what they expected, perhaps the creature should put in an appearance or two. Nothing like the threat from without to make folks more vulnerable to a threat from within.

He could use this to his advantage. The monster would deal more mercifully with an interloper than would the organization.

48

Chapter 6

Carly fidgeted in her seat in the doctor's waiting room, trying to remember the last time she'd sat here. Had to have been years. She was rarely sick. Didn't like going to doctors, particularly, preferring to tough it out, as her mother would say.

Mike sat beside her, calmly thumbing through a Christmas edition of a fishing magazine.

And likely not this past Christmas, either.

The rest of the chairs remained empty, either a testament to the otherwise healthy nature of the town's inhabitants, or the fact Mike procured the first appointment of the day.

In which case, why were they still sitting here at—she glanced at her cell phone—nine-thirty-two?

Goodness, was the doctor only two minutes late? Felt like she'd sat here for at least an hour.

The door leading into the offices at the rear opened. The kindly, older gentleman who'd been doctoring the inhabitants of Bear Cove for about a hundred years stepped out. His white medical coat and the stethoscope hanging around his neck gave him a Dr. Marcus Welby look, and the blue eyes wrapped in laugh wrinkles warmed her heart.

He nodded to her and Mike then returned to her. "You ready?"

She stood. "I'd like if Mike could come, too."

"Sure, sure. The more the merrier, I always say." He led them to an examination room off a hallway and gestured Mike to take the chair.

49

"You hop up on the table, if you don't mind."

Stifling a nervous giggle—the last time she hopped anywhere was when she stepped on a thumbtack that fell on the floor of her office last year—she clambered up. "I wish the table height was more suited to my short legs rather than to that of a basketball player."

Dr. Walsh chuckled. "Maybe I need a step stool."

Straightening her blouse and smoothing the front of her jeans, she drew two breaths. Dr. Walsh scanned her medical file, lips pursed, glasses perched halfway down his nose. "Been a while since I saw you. Nothing in your file shows any long-lasting issues. So, what is troubling you today?"

She glanced at Mike then turned back to the medic. "It's probably nothing, but I've had a few things going on for a couple of months now."

The doctor peered at her. "Couple of months, you say? Such as?"

Carly ran through the list of ways her body had been betraying her since before Christmas. A little here, a little there. But all adding up to a worrisome cocktail of potential symptoms. She smiled. "I'm sure you're going to tell me it's nothing. Or that I need more exercise. Or I work too much."

His smile calmed her fears like a soothing balm. "I'm not going into any discussion with you about increasing your heart rate, young lady. And really, I could explain away any one of these symptoms, on their own. Even two or three, particularly if they were of a short duration. Like up to a week." He pulled his stethoscope from around his neck. "But this is quite the catalogue. Let's start with listening to your heart and lungs."

Once satisfied both were working properly, he checked her eyes, ears, throat, then moved on to tapping her elbows, knees, and ankles. Without commenting, other than the customary "hmm" or "uh-huh" that all doctors seemed to learn in their first year of medical school.

Next he instructed her to follow his finger with her eyes only, without moving her head. Held up fingers for her to say how many. Moved said fingers until she couldn't see them any longer. Helped her down from the table and instructed her to travel a straight line without using her arms for balance. Balance first on one foot then the other. Tilt her head back and count backwards from one hundred by threes. Asked about her family medical history regarding various illnesses such as cancer, diabetes, stroke, heart attacks, to name a few.

Finally, he assisted her onto the table, his mouth turned down. He pulled a prescription pad from his jacket pocket and a pen from his shirt. "I'm going to write you a script—"

She held up a hand. "I don't want a drug to relieve symptoms. I want to know what's wrong with me."

"Well, that's just it. I'm not going to suggest a medication. At least, not right now."

She glanced at Mike. This sounded serious. "Not right now?"

Dr. Walsh exhaled. "Like I said. But I want you to get some tests done. Today. Starting with blood work, then an MRI."

Mike stood beside her. "What is it, Doc?"

"Not sure. Sometimes we get the answer through a test that tells us definitively what the problem is. Cancers are that way. Blood diseases. But sometimes we look at the overall picture, the package deal, you might say. Certain clusters of symptoms are diagnostics of certain diseases."

Carly gripped her husband's hand. "And which do you think this is?"

"I want to rule out what's easy. Make sure there are no arterial blockages. No brain or heart damage that could indicate minor strokes. No deficiencies such as anemia, vitamin or mineral."

"And if all that is negative?"

He sat behind his desk, giving her the distinct impression he wanted to put distance between himself and the diagnosis. Jotted notes in her medical file. Then removed his glasses and folded them before tucking them into his jacket chest pocket. "I suspect you have MS."

+ + +

Following the pronouncement from Doc Walsh, Mike suggested an early lunch, which Carly agreed to. Any excuse not to cook was a good one—although she could have skipped the entire office visit and dire initial diagnosis, going instead directly to food.

When Mike pulled into their driveway and parked, he exited the

51

car and came around to open her door. She resisted stepping out before he got there, even though everything within her screamed she wasn't sick. She wasn't disabled. She could open her own car door. No, that was simply Mike. A gentleman in the old-fashioned sense of the word.

For which she was immensely grateful.

Particularly today. She stared at the latch as he rounded the front of the car. Her brain failed to connect with her fingers to tell them what to do. She snorted. That was dumb. Not remembering how to open the car door. What next? Forgetting how to tie her shoes?

Well, that wasn't about to happen.

She hated laces. Always chose loafers, slip-ons, or hook-and-loop fasteners. Especially on shoes.

She stepped out and wrapped her arms around his waist, pulling him close. Inhaling his warm Mike-smell. Feeling safe in his embrace. She could stay here all day.

When Carly stepped inside her front door, everything looked different. Not in any particular way she could describe or communicate. Was that the fault of an insidious disease that threatened her life? Or was it merely because this threat opened her eyes to what was really important?

She collapsed onto the sofa while Mike brought in several bags of groceries she insisted they purchase, despite his protests that no matter the outcome, she wouldn't be incapacitated within the next few days. Shopping could wait, he insisted.

But she won out. As she usually did.

Perhaps, given what the future might hold for her, for them, she should change her ways. Be less insistent on having her way, more cognizant of how she treated others. Choose sympathy and compassion over a quick comeback and a sharp tongue. Leave Mike with sweet memories of their final years, months, or days together.

Get her affairs in order.

There, she'd said it. Not out loud, of course, because she couldn't quite bring herself to utter those words yet. But soon. If Doc Walsh was right—and he likely was after so many years—her physical and mental condition would deteriorate on an exponentially downward curved basis. A little at a time, more noticeable over the months, until—

She shivered and pulled the afghan around her shoulders. She wouldn't go there. Not yet.

Mike entered and closed the door, carrying two more bags of groceries. "Are you cold? I'll turn up the heat."

The temperature of the house wasn't her problem. He knew it and so did she. But she smiled and let him do his thing, turning up the thermostat in the hallway before heading to the kitchen. He rustled through the bags, placing a few items in the fridge or freezer, before returning to the living room and sitting beside her.

"We've had a busy day."

She nodded and leaned against him. "That we have."

"Mysteries of all kinds."

She exhaled. "Maybe I'd have been better off not knowing."

He shifted away and held her at arm's length. "That is not the answer. Now we can make adjustments, preparations, for whatever is coming."

She shook her head and her vision blurred. Only this time, tears were the cause. "I don't know."

"I do. When my father died of his first heart attack, my mother told me she wished she'd had more notice so she could relish their last days together. Instead, all she could remember was how she pestered him to get up and get moving in his last days. She thought he was being lazy, not understanding he was sick. He didn't understand what was happening either, and went through depression, self-chastisement. Even suicidal thoughts. When all along it was his heart."

"I guess you're right. But I don't understand. I thought MS happened to young women in the prime of their youth."

"As Doc Walsh explained, also to men, but a small percentage. And sometimes the symptoms are overlooked, or minimal, early on. And once in a while, it happens to us older folks."

A tear slipped down her cheek. "I don't want to be a burden to you. Or to drain our life savings and leave you with nothing for retirement."

He hugged her close again, and she melted into his arms. "That won't happen. We have decent health insurance. And we'll make these decisions together."

She pulled away and stared up at his strong nose, the dimple in his chin. "And when I can't make those decisions?"

"We'll cross that bridge if we come to it." He kissed the top of her head. "For now, we're both tired. I'll warm up leftovers and make hot chocolate, then it's early to bed for both of us."

"That sounds good. Maybe ice cream?"

"Rest your weary bones here for a bit." He kissed the end of her nose. "And if you're obedient, maybe we'll splurge today."

She laid her head back on the sofa and closed her eyes while he put away the rest of the groceries then started their snack. Knowing Mike, he'd also put together a salad from the kit they purchased.

Faces flashed across her mind. Tom and Sarah. Bradley. Denise and Don. Margie and Toby. Those people most important in her life. Who she'd need to share what was going on with her.

The thought of calling and breaking such devastating news over the phone wearied her. But would it come any easier in person? Over a meal? And if she called and asked everybody to gather over the weekend, they'd suspect something was up. Maybe think it had to do with Mike. Perhaps come to the C-word conclusion.

She rolled her eyes. Since when would receiving a cancer diagnosis be better than the alternative? Since there was no cure for MS, no magical surgery to remove it, no potion to slow it.

At this point, almost any cancer would be a relief. Chemo, radiation, and surgery, along with long-term cancer cocktails, were re-writing the prognoses for most types of cancer these days.

Funny how twenty-four hours could change everything. Yesterday, if told she might have cancer, she'd never have felt relief.

But today. . .

Then another face, and another, crossed her mind. Victoria. Mrs. Olsen. The pastor at the church. After spending time with Steve and

Loretta in Colorado last fall, she'd returned to Bear Cove with a different perspective on faith and religion and its place in her life. Went to church a few times to sort of try it on for size, but didn't quite see how she fit in— or how faith fit into her life, either.

Sure, Denise and Don and the kids encouraged her to keep at it. When they missed three Sundays because of other things on her calendar, she and Mike decided not to go back. In fact, he seemed as relieved as she was not to attend.

But faced with the prospect of after spending an hour inside the MRI machine, along with a plethora of other tests, she was rethinking her position.

If the only time she turned to God was when things were tough, she'd need Him more than ever in the coming months. And years. If Doc Walsh was right.

"Hey, Mike?"

He stood in the doorway between the kitchen and dining room, wiping his hands on a towel. "Yeah?"

"Want to go to church on Sunday?"

He chuckled. "Are you a mind reader?"

"What do you mean?"

"I was thinking the same thing. Maybe we didn't give it enough time before."

"Like it has to grow on us or something?"

He turned back to the kitchen. "Something like that."

Well, if that's what was needed, she'd give God some time.

At least, whatever time she had left.

+ + +

Interesting how when a person faced a challenge in their everyday life, turning to the supernatural wasn't uncommon. In America, as well as Peru, apparently. Well, these people could turn to their own god as much as they wanted. He wouldn't be able to help them if they got in the way.

Not even *El Chullachaqui* could stop the organization. Although this mythical creature would prove useful, no doubt.

Plans were well underway for the successful conclusion of this assignment. There was no room for failure, and interlopers were dealt with severely. Just look at the thief who tried to extract precious artifacts from his own country.

And now rumors of sightings and hints of a secret society filled the media in Peru. This was good. Create fear, promulgate suspicions, and soon fathers would turn in their own children. Which is the way it should be regarding the theft of cultural artifacts for profit or personal gain.

Isn't that why the organization was founded almost five hundred years ago? To stop what the conquistadors began, and to return objects stolen by them. In fact, the first group of men assigned this important task hid the treasures in the holy city of Machu Picchu. When the Spanish invaded, they blocked the trails to protect it from looting. Commissioned by the ailing Quechuan king, Atahuallpa, before his execution by the hated Spaniards, then sworn to secrecy and empowered with replenishing their ranks until the Quechuan returned to power.

Yes, Atahuallpa's promise to return one day was enough to strengthen for the day at hand. Nothing would stop the holy king's plan.

Nothing.

And nobody.

Chapter 7

Thursday morning found Carly cooling her heels once again in a medical office.

And the fact Mike sat beside her, head leaned against the wall and snoring, didn't help much. Snoring! How could the man sleep at a time like this? In minutes, she'd lie on a cold plastic table, her hospital gown gaping at the back. Then a conveyor-belt mechanism would roll her into an electronic tube that would penetrate her body with mysterious rays.

According to research she did earlier that morning when she couldn't sleep and didn't want to wake Mike, her upcoming procedure would be painless but perhaps claustrophobic. Images on the Internet showed a long, narrow tube, open at both ends. The machine would emit a strong magnetic field and radio waves that magically produced an image that a radiologist would later interpret.

The door at the far end of the waiting room opened, and a frail-looking woman in a wheelchair pushed by an aide entered. The patient hunched in the chair, a blanket over her knees and a turban around her head.

Carly nodded when the woman smiled in her direction, then berated herself for her errant thoughts. She had nothing to complain about compared to others.

At least, nothing she knew about.

If and when she did, well, that would be soon enough to gripe.

The door to the radiology room opened, and a young woman

attired in cheerful polka-dot-covered scrubs stepped out, a clipboard in hand. Her nametag read KATE "Mrs. Turnquist?"

Carly stood. "That's me."

"Follow me, please."

"I'll be right with you, Kate." Carly nudged her husband. "Mike, they're calling me."

He bounded to his feet. "Quick hug for courage."

He pulled her against him, and heat raced up her cheeks. She didn't mind public displays of affection that weren't quite so—well, public. She enjoyed holding hands as they strolled, and she wasn't averse to hugging or even kissing politely in front of the kids and grands.

However, before strangers, and particularly the woman in the wheelchair—well, *unseemly* is how her mother would have described the behavior.

She planted a kiss on his cheek then pushed away. "Don't want to keep them waiting."

He released her. "Right." A soft clearing of his throat accompanied the duck of his head. "I'll be waiting for you right here."

She turned and followed the radiology tech into the room, and the door swished shut behind her, cutting her off from her normal world.

Kate led the way to a table beside a machine as large as a Volkswagen. "Hop up here on this table, Mrs. Turnquist."

"Carly, please. Mrs. Turnquist is Mike's mother."

In fact, every time she heard the phrase, she turned, expecting to see the woman, who'd been dead for several years, behind her.

While she loved Mike, his mother had been a bit of a tyrant.

Kate nodded. "Carly it is. Did the doctor explain the procedure?"

"Not really."

Carly tied her fingers into knots. Her hands might as well resemble her stomach. Maybe she should have asked for a few minutes to hit the washroom before coming in. She glanced around. The closing of the door seemed so final. Like Hotel California. Once she came in, there was no escape. And what was it about this machine? Its gaping maw looked well able to chew her up and not even burp.

Kate patted the table. "No worries. I'll give you a rundown, and if you have questions, ask away."

Carly sat on the bench-like contraption, her mind buzzing with questions such as: Will it hurt? Will I be able to walk out of here under my own power? What are the cancer risks? How does it work?

However, within a few minutes, Kate answered all of her questions. And more. No, it wouldn't hurt. In fact, she wouldn't feel a thing. And yes, she would exit the room as she entered. No known cancer risks. And the device took photographs of slices of her brain.

Kate's smile never slipped once as she concluded her spiel. "Some people admit to feeling a little claustrophobic, so we recommend you wear these headphones and keep your eyes closed." She held up a stereo-quality headset. "We can dial in calming music of your choice."

"Got ocean waves or rain forest? Something like that?"

"Actually, music is better. I love those sound tracks, too, but they don't cover the noise of the machine well enough, so we recommend something with a melody you can focus on."

"Noise?"

"Yes. The device makes various sounds throughout the process, including a jackhammer, a loud clicking like a magnified camera sound, birds chirping, and a sort of gonging alarm sound."

None of which she wanted inside her head this morning, for sure.

She nodded. "Headset it is." She pondered her choices a moment. "How about Celtic music? And I'll try to keep my toes from dancing."

Kate smiled. "Excellent choice. And thanks for showing restraint. We need you to stay as still as possible."

Ten minutes later, Carly lay prone on the table, headphones blocking out all sound, a strange contraption like a football helmet around her head, and a pillow beneath her knees while Kate pressed various buttons. The table rose level with the machine, and she slid inside. Despite the instruction to keep her eyes closed, she resisted. She was a full believer in the theory that if she could see it, it wouldn't kill her.

However, her toes tickled to wiggle, so she shut her eyes and concentrated on remaining still. Kate mentioned—offhandedly as though this little detail was of no consequence—that her time inside the device would be thirty minutes. Well, that was a long time to lie in one position with Ceilidh music filling her head.

Hopefully, the sound waves didn't show up on the MRI.

Once the soundtrack filled with fiddles and flutes reached the end of its loop and played the first song again, however, Carly was ready for this to end. A quick peek at the surrounding tube confirmed the wisdom of her decision to keep her eyes closed.

A series of loud hammer-like concussions overwhelmed the fine music, and she gritted her teeth. A little warning would be good.

Then the pounding ended, and the table eased out the way it went in. Carly glanced into the mirror on the helmet-like frame and smiled. Kate stood in place awaiting her return.

A minute later and she sat up and exhaled. "Well, that wasn't as bad as I'd envisioned."

Not completely true. A few more minutes, and she might have pressed the panic button Kate placed in her right hand before the test began, assuring her that if she wanted to stop the procedure, she could at any time.

Kate's bright smile filled the room. "Good to hear. Dr. Tess, the radiologist, will send the results to your doctor." She checked the clipboard in her hand. "Dr. Walsh. And he'll call you once he receives them and make an appointment to communicate the results. That will probably take a couple of days."

Well, that was a little disappointing. "So, no chance of Dr. Tess telling me anything today?"

"Sorry. No. You could get a call as early as Monday, though." Kate offered her hand, and Carly stood. "Hope I don't see you again."

Carly nodded. "I bet you say that to all your patients."

"I do, actually. Well, not if I'm already aware of their diagnosis, of course."

Carly's mind cast back to the cancer patient in the waiting room. "Understood."

A few more days of uncertainty before she knew whether Dr.

Walsh's initial assessment was correct.

Maybe this was a case where not knowing was better than the alternative.

+ + +

By noon that afternoon, Carly questioned the wisdom of her theory on not knowing. She had two mysteries on her plate at the same time, and the lack of facts and needed answers to the questions so she could solve said conundrums was driving her to distraction.

Or was that another symptom of her diagnosis?

Over lunch, when she told Mike about the expected appointment next week, he nodded. "But for your own peace of mind, no more MS research until we meet the doctor." He hugged her close. "After all, if you ask where Jimmy Hoffa is buried, you'll get many conflicting answers."

"Understood." She chuckled. "Sounds like firsthand experience."

"I will admit to wasting a few boring hours one rainy afternoon exploring the question."

She slid her remaining half a sandwich across the kitchen table toward him. "Finish that for me?"

"Sure."

"So, what you're saying is that simply because it's on the Internet, doesn't mean it's true?"

He chewed and swallowed, washing the mouthful down with coffee. "Right. Couldn't have said it better myself." He reached across the table and held her hand. "There will be plenty of time to figure what steps to take next once we talk to Doc Walsh."

"You're right."

He smiled and pulled out his cell phone, tapped buttons, then turned the device off.

"And what was that about?"

"Just wanted to note for posterity's sake that you said I was right about something."

She shook her head. "You're trying to distract me."

"True. But I learned a long time ago that if I couldn't change a situation, I might as well leave it be and find something else to focus on."

61

She considered his words for a moment then nodded. "I see what you mean. I'll focus on Amanda's Peruvian mystery and leave my personal enigma by the wayside. For now."

He finished her leftovers, stood, and carried their plates to the sink. "I'll look after those later. For now, you have a choice."

"Oh? And what might that be?"

"I can take you to bed, or into the office."

While working from home had its benefits—including flexible schedules and opportunities for relaxation not afforded those who worked in an office—that was about the most unromantic proposition he'd ever dangled before her.

Her brow pulled down. "Mike Turnquist. . . "

He tilted his head in question, then chuckled. "No. No eyebrow waggling going on here, I promise you. But Doc Walsh said that you should rest whenever you felt the need."

"I'm not wasting any more time today. I have work to do. I can always go to bed early if I want."

He held out his arm, and she hooked hers through his. "This way, milady."

As much as she detested admitting she might need help, she gripped his arm. Leaving the hospital, she'd stumbled twice, catching herself the first time on a handrail, and on Mike's arm on the second instance. And then, getting out of the car, she forgot to unfasten her seatbelt, which left her in an embarrassing web until Mike released the buckle.

Safely seated at her desk, she considered her next move. After a glance at her notes, she determined a phone call to Customs was in order. She dug out the copy of the bill of lading from the package delivered to Amanda's shop and checked for the customs office number and the inspector identification before dialing.

As she waited for the officer to answer, she thumbed through the rest of her notes and papers, including an article about the jungle monster. She shook her head at the gullibility of people, then recalled how entire economies were based on such myths. Nessie the Loch Ness monster. Big

Foot and Sasquatch. The Abominable Snowman in the Himalayas. Seemed people wanted to believe in something.

Was that the same with God? Was religion merely an invention to answers those difficult questions about life and death and purpose? Don and Denise didn't believe that. Nor did the millions of believers around the world and throughout history.

But did a large following automatically grant authority? Couldn't those millions be completely convinced *and* also be completely wrong?

Not knowing enough facts to prove or disprove the validity of religion, she waited while loud classical music played in her ear. At one point, she checked the digital readout on the face of the handset. Twelve minutes. Was that all? She felt like she'd been waiting for at least an hour.

Just when she was about ready to hang up and try another time, a male voice answered. "Gibbons, Customs Officer ID 98-410. How can I help you?"

Carly introduced herself. "I'm working for Amanda Bartlett. She owns a business here in Bear Cove, Maine." She filled Officer Gibbons in on details about the re-taped package and the missing items. "You see, Officer Gibbons, we were told the package went through Customs without drawing any attention."

A lengthy sigh. "Got the lading number?"

Carly read off the details. "The package cleared your office a week ago. And I don't expect you to have any recollection of the package."

The man laughed, a scratchy, gravelly sound like he didn't chuckle often enough. "You're right there. I inspect hundreds of packages from all over the world every day." The clickety-clack of keys in the back heralded his digital search. "I have the information. Uh-huh. Same package weight as at ParcelExpress office in Cusco. Contents listed as jewelry for retail sale in the US, so I calculated the excise and charged the account." More clicking. "Yep, appears your client imports a fair bit. She already has an account set up, so I charged that off."

"Would there be any video of the package after it left your station?"

"Maybe ParcelExpress has some. Like I said, the items were all

63

accounted for here."

"And where are you, exactly, so I know where to start?"

"In Bangor."

"Wow. There are direct flights from Cusco to Bangor? Who'd'a thought?"

Another chuckle. "No, the package went to Panama City from Cusco, then changed planes and came directly to Bangor from there. I handled it because it's the first port of entry in the US on the package's journey."

"So, then it you transferred it to ParcelExpress again?"

"Well, theoretically it never left ParcelExpress purview. Packages come into the country in boxes or bags owned by each express company and stay under their jurisdiction until delivered. You could check with their warehouse here in Bangor, though. They'd probably have video until the point they separated it to the truck delivering on the route to your town. Bean Cove, was it?"

She gritted her teeth. "Bear Cove."

He guffawed outright this time. "Easy mistake. Bet you hear it all the time, eh?"

Yeah. Usually because the offender didn't bother to listen. She pasted on a smile she hoped transmitted through the telephone line. "Thank you, Office Gibbons. Have a great day."

She disconnected the call, no wiser than before she'd invested—a glance at the clock—almost thirty minutes to learn nothing new.

Almost as big a waste of time as the MRI earlier today.

Except that the results of *that* investment were still to be determined.

+ + +

Good. Everything is in place for the mission for tonight. Black pants and sweater. Black balaclava. Black shoes. Purchasing these items in four different shopping trips to the big box retailer up on the highway consumed most of the day. Particularly since that store had no self check-outs and few cashiers. So as not to draw attention, I wasted hours waiting for one woman's shift to end before paying for the last item.

64

Still, my time was not completely wasted, since the store also boasted a fast-food outlet where I bought a giant hamburger and a milkshake. Sat and ate the meal. For an outrageous price, of course. With the same amount of money in Peru, an entire family could eat for two or three days.

Just another example of how America wasted so many valuable resources. In this case, money.

A glance around the motel room confirms all is ready. The outfit. The lock-picking tools. A black backpack. And *El Chullachaqui*, complete with a booted foot and an animal extremity. Not a goat, but in this area, there weren't any opportunities for such. Instead, a cow hoof would suffice, rummaged from the dumpster behind a butcher shop in the next town.

Still, beggars couldn't be choosers.

And begging was not on the agenda.

Getting what belonged to Peru was.

And soon. Tonight. After the shop closed.

Success was imminent.

Chapter 8

When the telephone rang early the next morning—very early, even before the sun was up—Carly groaned and rolled over. Who in their right mind was calling her at this hour?

She snagged the handset on the third ring. "Hello?"

"Carly?"

Amanda. "No, it's Santa Claus, and you've got the wrong number." She raised herself up on her elbow, turning her shoulder so she didn't disturb Mike. Once awakened, he'd be up, showering, blow-drying his hair, and raising all sorts of ruckus. At—she opened one eye and glared at the clock radio on the bedside table—twenty-three minutes past five. "What do you want, Amanda?"

"My shop was broken into."

Now that was news worth hearing. She tucked her toes into her fluffy slippers and crept out of the bedroom and down the hallway. "When?"

"About an hour ago. The silent alarm sounded at the police department, but by the time the officer on call arrived, the thief was gone." The shopkeeper spoke to somebody in the background. "I'm here now. They want a list of what the thief took." A broken sob interrupted the conversation. "How am I supposed to figure that out? I don't take inventory every day."

"Give me ten minutes. I'll get dressed and meet you there. I'll help you figure out what's going on."

A hiccup and a sniffle. "Okay. It's not like I have anywhere else to go anyway."

Right. And me neither. Carly disconnected the call and snuck back into the bedroom. After dressing, she brushed her teeth and her hair, then headed for the front door, grabbing her keys along the way.

Then she paused. Mike didn't want her driving alone until they knew what was going on with her neurologically. She glanced at the clock on the mantle. But if she woke him now to drive her, he'd take another ten minutes, and Amanda would gripe at her for being so late. Likely make a snide comment that Carly's toilette shouldn't take but a fraction of the time, given the results. Or something like that.

Then again, it wasn't even six in the morning—who knew there was such a thing?—and she *was* doing this as a favor to Amanda.

She sighed. She'd choose domestic bliss over friendship any day.

Carly scurried back to the bedroom and shook Mike's shoulder. "Wake up. I need you to drive me—"

He grunted, opened one eye, then bolted out of bed, snatching his trousers from the chair beside the bed where he tossed them the night before. "To the hospital? Are you okay?" He gripped her hand and pressed her onto the now-vacant chair. "Give me a minute and—"

"Mike. I'm okay. Slow down."

"You said you needed me to drive you—"

"Yes. To Amanda's shop."

His shirt slid down over his head, his arms up in the air like he was being held at gunpoint. "Her shop?" He checked the clock. "At five-thirty in the morning?"

"She called. Said somebody broke in. Please hurry."

He nodded and rammed his feet into a pair of loafers, picked up a windbreaker in one hand and grabbed her hand with the other, then led the way to the front door. One thing she could say about Mike, once set on a direction, there was no stopping him.

In the car, he started the engine and waited until she buckled in before backing out of the driveway. The wipers swept away the early morning fog and mist, and Carly wished they could do the same for her own brain fog. A symptom of MS? Or merely the result of being woken so early and now being expected to operate on a higher cerebral level without even a sip of coffee in her system?

"So, tell me more about why we're on the streets so early."

Mike's words broke into her daydreams of a bathtub-sized mug of java. "I know little more than I told you. She said the shop was burgled about an hour ago, but the police didn't get there in time to catch anybody."

"What would a small dress shop in an even smaller town in Maine have that would attract a thief? It's not like she has high-end products or something."

Carly chuckled. "Don't let her hear you say that. She considers all her wares highest quality." She stared out the side window, swiping at the condensation so she could see. "But you're right. She said her highest priced jewelry comes in at around two hundred dollars. And that would be for a very nice piece. Her dresses are more expensive, up to around five hundred."

"No wonder you always buy off the sale rack."

"Well, that would be for a nice evening gown. Or a special order wedding dress." She and Mike thought more alike than he'd want to admit. The same question had tumbled around her noggin ever since the call. "I told her I'd help her figure out what was missing."

Mike made the turn onto Main Street and eased into a parking space beside a police cruiser—one of the town's two—in front of the shop. Apart from the single emergency vehicle, the street was quiet. None of the other businesses opened until at least seven. Even the Dew Drop Inn's front-of-the-store lights were off, although no doubt Victoria and the cook were likely busy preparing for the opening rush.

Carly unbuckled her seat belt—no getting caught up like the last time. Maybe she was getting better. Was it possible to recover from something like MS over a weekend? And if it wasn't that dire diagnosis, perhaps a flu bug or not enough sleep was the culprit?

She sighed. If lack of sleep was the cause, she hadn't done herself any favors. This morning's early rise wouldn't add to her healing.

Mike opened the door, and she planted a kiss on his cheek, smiling up at his unruly hair. "I'll call when I'm ready to be picked up."

He peered at her. "I think I'll stay. What if the thief comes back?"

Her heart thudded to her toes. She hadn't considered that possibility. "That would be nice. I'd feel safer if you were here."

Together they entered the shop, nodding to Police Chief Donovan who nodded to them from a display case near the cash register.

He met them in the middle of the store. "Carly. Mike. Funny meeting you here. 'Specially at this hour." He peered at her, his dark eyes boring into her skull. "Speaking of which, what are you doing here?"

Mike sidled half a step closer to the officer, effectively placing her behind him. She gritted her teeth. Like she needed protecting or couldn't speak for herself. "Amanda hired her to check into a business matter and called Carly about the burglary."

Donovan's brows raised. "So, are the two events related?"

Carly stepped around her husband. "What two events?"

"The missing items from the package, and now the break-in." He sneered. "She didn't tell you she reported the original theft to us?"

"No, she neglected to mention that."

"Well, you're not the only investigator in town."

"Florida's loss, I'm sure." The chief moved to town a year or so prior, and while he—and Officer Adam Meyers—proved invaluable to solving the mystery in Colorado the previous year, that didn't mean they would ever be bosom buddies. "Find anything to identify the thief?"

He nodded toward Officer Meyers, who dabbed a fingerprint brush over the cash register. "Not yet. Of course, it's early days."

She offered her most insincere smile to compliment his—half sneer, half smirk. "And as we all know, the first two days are critical to solving a case." She peered up at her husband. "Statistics prove that cases unsolved after forty-eight hours are five times more likely to languish in the cold cases file."

Chief Donovan sighed. "Watching *Forensic Files* again, are we, Carly? And we all know how realistic those programs are."

Amanda entered the store from the work area at the rear of the

70

shop. "Oh, Carly." She hurried across the floor, her heels tapping on the hardwood, and grabbed Carly in a full-on bear hug. "I thought you'd never get here. I was so scared. I don't know what to do. I feel so violated." She buried her face in Carly's shoulder and sobbed. "Please help me. I think I'm losing my mind."

With her arms pinned to her sides—she hadn't expected the woman's effusive gesture, so hadn't prepared to defend herself, as it were—Carly could do little but stand there, offering small murmurs of encouragement. All the while, her head screamed silently for Amanda to release her. Or for Mike to interrupt. Or for a bolt of lightning to slash through the ceiling and break up this most unwelcome hug.

Instead, her nemesis, the chief, cleared his throat. "Miss Bartlett, I have a few more questions."

The shop owner stiffened at his words then released her captive, and Carly moved out of reach. "I'm happy to help, but I can't think what else you need."

Mike smiled at the frazzled woman. "I make a mean pot of coffee. Point me in the right direction, and I'll get out from under your feet."

Amanda gestured toward the work room before addressing Chief Donovan. "What else do you need to ask?"

Carly followed along in Mike's wake. "Thanks for rescuing me."

"I didn't realize you and Amanda were so tight."

She held her finger over her mouth in the universal sign to hush. Once behind the curtain separating the retail area from the back room, she pressed her ear to the fabric. At a tap on her shoulder, she turned.

"What are you doing?"

She resumed listening to the conversation going on in the other room. "What does it look like I'm doing?"

"Eavesdropping, my dear. Not nice."

She groaned. "Make the coffee, will you? And leave me to sleuthing." She straightened when Amanda's heels once again tip-tapped on the floor. This time in her direction. "That's it, Mike. The coffee goes in the little basket thingy. Just like the one at home." She turned when the shop owner stepped through the curtain. "Oh, Amanda, there you are.

Where do you want me to start?"

"I don't know. Really, I don't."

Amanda ran fingers through her hair, disturbing the previously perfect coiffure. How could a woman, roused out of bed so early and under such distressing circumstances, have remembered to style her hair?

Or perhaps she'd already been up.

Burglarizing her own shop.

But for what purpose? And, not to toot her own horn or anything, but why call her in if that was the case? Kind of like an arsonist calling the fire department and asking them to find him.

Carly directed the woman to a nearby chair. "Tell me what you've done already, and I'll pick up from there."

That was something Amanda was good at—telling other people what to do.

"I don't leave cash in the register. It's in the safe. And it's all there. Along with the more expensive pieces. The display cases are untouched. And Chief Donovan said there were no fingerprints anywhere. Which means the thief wiped down all the surfaces before he left."

This was an odd piece of information. Why not simply wear gloves? Unless the thief had been in the shop prior without his or her hands being covered. Had he or she—really, all this gender neutral thinking gave her a headache. Most likely the criminal was a man. Time to think of him as such. The question remained, had the thief reconnoitered the store during business hours, perhaps even admired a particular piece, then returned to steal it?

Or was there something else going on?

"Who has been in the store in the past few days?"

Amanda rubbed at her temple. "Let me think. Well, me, of course. And you and Mike. And the police."

"Think back before today. Who was here yesterday?"

"Half of the women in Bear Cove. I received a new shipment, so I made a few phone calls, hung an announcement in the front window."

Half of Bear Cove indeed. Amanda might wish that were true. "Anybody you didn't recognize?"

72

"There were at least four carloads of women from outside town who always shop here." Amanda eyed Carly up and down. No doubt the jeans and sweatshirt she'd hastily donned didn't exactly fit the woman's customer demographics. "I know them by name, of course."

"Anyone else?" She sipped the coffee Mike handed her. Delish— exactly what she needed. "The day before?"

"Regulars. A couple of lookie-lous from the county. And the ParcelExpress driver, of course."

Mike pressed a cup into the woman's hands. "Drink this. You are chilled to the bone."

"More from fright than the temperature." She gazed around the room. "Why is this happening to me?"

Wait a minute. Amanda said — "Who was the driver?"

She shrugged. "Some man."

"Did he who deliver the package from Peru?"

Amanda straightened and set her cup aside, her hand shaking. "Yes. Why?"

"Was it Victor?"

Amanda closed her eyes a moment. "Now that you mention it, no. It was another man."

"Did you notice his nametag?"

A quick shake of the head. "Who notices these things? I was busy. I had a customer in the fitting room, and another at the sale rack. I signed for the package and got him out of the way before the woman grew roots." She rolled her eyes. "Like some people I could name, who never buy at regular price."

"Was he wearing gloves?"

"How do I know that? Why would I notice if he did or not? He came in, set the package on the counter, and gave me the digital pad to sign." She sighed. "Although why they bother, I cannot fathom. Those things never work right. Took me a couple of tries. And all the while my customers are cooling their heels, and he's—"

"He's what?"

"Looking at the display case in front of the window. Where I

73

place the pieces from Peru." She stood and headed that direction, through the curtain, into the retail area, now devoid of any police officers. "He rested his hands on top, like this." She mimicked the man's actions, palms down on the glass. "I remember now. I asked him if he saw anything he liked, and he said no, but he appreciated the artistry of the Quechuan workmanship."

Carly checked out the display. "There's nothing here that mentions the specific origin. Just this little sign that says the pieces were handmade in Peru." She peered at Amanda. "That's a very specific detail, don't you think?"

The woman sniffed. "Obviously, he has discerning tastes. Even if he is only a delivery driver."

"Who delivered your package in less than complete condition. Maybe that's important?"

Amanda's eyes and mouth widened. "You don't think—" She shook her head and backed away. "You mean, I was in the same room as the burglar?"

"I don't know for sure, but it would explain why there are no fingerprints. There should be. Yours should be here, for example, unless you make it a habit of wiping down every surface before you leave for the day."

"Goodness, no. I have a cleaner who comes in, but she's not due for a few days."

"Then given the amount of traffic you mentioned, this place should be crawling with fingerprints."

Amanda shuddered. "Ooh, don't use that term in my shop. I assure you, nothing crawls in here."

Carly was fairly certain no self-respecting insect would dare show its face in this shop, that was for sure. "What else did Chief Donovan want to ask you?"

"Nothing, really. He wanted to assure me he would do everything to solve this case and set my mind at ease. Said he'd need a list of anything missing and asked that I keep him in the loop on whatever we find on the other matter."

"Other matter?" Carly's ears perked up. "You mean the missing samples?"

"I assume so."

"Does he think the two are related?"

Amanda shrugged. "He didn't say." She paused and squinted. "Which is strange."

"What is?"

"When I originally called to tell him the package was tampered with, he wasn't really interested. Said I should take it up with the express company and have the sender claim it through their insurance."

"But suddenly he wants in?"

Except, not really in, since he didn't want to do any of the work. Typical.

Amanda turned from the window. "Not that it's important. And I guess I might have mentioned the murder in Peru. That's when he really perked up. But let's do a quick inventory and make a list of what was taken."

An hour later, Amanda's list was as long as when they started.

Nothing.

That's what the thief stole.

Unless she counted the fingerprints. But was that worth risking capture?

Perhaps. If the driver who said his name was Nate didn't want the police to know he was in town. Except what was the likelihood his fingerprints would have been discovered and identified if he hadn't burgled the shop? No, if that's why he broke in, he succeeded only in drawing attention to himself.

What else was in the shop that he wanted? Not the samples. He—or somebody else—already had them. Something else in the package? Why didn't he take it when he had the chance? Why even deliver the rest of the contents? In fact, if he'd taken the entire thing, nobody would have been the wiser that his actual goal was the samples. Rogelio would have placed a claim with the express delivery company, who would have reimbursed him for the value, and everybody concerned would have carried on as usual.

Unless maybe something was already missing from the package? Was a second shipment sent containing additional items? Is that what he sought?

"Amanda, how often do you get deliveries from Rogelio?"

Another shrug. "Every month or so."

"Does he ever split the orders so you get more than one package?"

"Sometimes an artisan hasn't completed an order, so Rogelio sends what he has, then ships the rest when he receives it."

"That's what happened with this particular package, right? Might there be a third shipment?"

Amanda's brow raised. "Oh, you mean the missing pieces might have shipped separately?" Her shoulders sagged. "No, Rogelio said he placed the samples in the same package."

"Maybe the thief thought there was another delivery. Had you received another package over than the two from Peru in recent days?"

"No, but some weeks I might." Amanda's fingers fluttered as she talked. "Victor is sometimes here three times a week."

"So, perhaps the crook came searching for other pieces?"

The woman wrapped her arms around herself as though warding off the chill. "If he didn't find what he sought, you mean he might come back?"

"Possibly. I think you should arrange to have somebody here with you at all times."

"But he didn't come this time during normal hours. He broke in at night."

"I'd feel better if I knew you were safe."

Amanda shriveled into herself. "I don't think I'll ever feel safe again."

+ + +

Carly snuggled into her afghan on the sofa, her latest mystery novel purchase in her lap. After an early rise, a stressful morning, and a boring afternoon where Mike wouldn't let her out of his sight, a few minutes to herself was exactly what she needed.

When she returned home, a message awaited her attention on the answering machine.

Her follow-up appointment with Doc Walsh to discuss the results of the MRI and the radiologist's report was for four o'clock Tuesday.

Thud!

Felt like another nail being driven into her coffin.

Still, she wouldn't give up. No way. She had far too much living to do yet. Time with the kids. Hugs from the grands. Moseying with Mike.

Okay, maybe not actual exercise. Snuggles with Mike. Books to read.

And a criminal to identify and capture. Not on her own, of course. No, Chief Donovan was the man for the actual takedown. But she could help in some small way.

If she could keep her eyes open.

With dinner done and cleared away more than an hour before, she had nothing ahead but a quiet night in. Maybe early to bed was in the cards for her. A hot bath first to release the tangled muscles at the base of her neck and in her shoulders, a pretty candle scenting the room—aah, heaven on earth.

She leaned her head back against the comfy pillow, her eyes drooping.

A sharp noise in the distance and she lifted her head, eyes wide, ears focused. What was that? A car backfiring? She relaxed again, inhaling and holding her breath to a count of five to slow her racing heart. Must be. Few in Bear Cove owned guns, and why would they—

Another. Like a loud pop. Fireworks? Possibly, but unlikely. Folks seldom lit fireworks except in July. And May. Sometimes in September.

Never in February.

An explosion? She sat up this time and folded the covering beside her, setting her book on the coffee table.

Footsteps in the hallway drew her attention, and Mike entered the room.

He peered through the curtain. "Did you hear that?"

"I did. Glad to know I'm not dreaming it."

She stood beside him. Nothing untoward on their street. She headed for the foyer and slipped on her shoes then pulled her jacket from the hook and grabbed her keys.

Mike barred her way through the door. "And where do you think you're going?"

"Out to see what's going on."

"Not without me, you aren't." He jammed his feet into his tennis shoes without stopping to untie them then donned his windbreaker. He held out his hand, palm up. "Keys, please."

"But Mike."

"No but Mike. I drive, or we stay home."

She glared at him for about half a second before handing over the keys. "Let's hurry. Sounds like it's downtown."

Within three minutes they made the turn onto Main Street and located the origin of the noise.

Jacob Roy's Garage.

Given the late hour, normally the business would be closed, along with the rest of the establishments in the main business core. And while beyond the garage, lights were off and shades drawn, not here.

In fact, with all the lights blazing, the lot was lit up like midday.

Or maybe the police cruiser's emergency and takedown lights created that impression.

Chief Donovan, wearing a crumpled overcoat and a slouch hat, stood near the gas pumps, his back to the street. Judging by the way he waved his hands, he sought to talk somebody into—or out of—a contrary course of action.

Mike pulled in as far from the scene of the altercation as he could and still be on garage property. He laid a hand on her arm. "Wait a minute. Let's see what's going on before we get ourselves caught in the middle of something we should stay out of."

Carly nodded, her eyes fixed on the scene before her. Appeared like the chief was trying to tell somebody—that person moved into her line of vision. "Jacob."

"What?" Mike peered around the rearview mirror. "What's that crazy old man up to now?"

Carly gasped, the words caught in her throat. "He—he's waving a gun around. Pointing across the street." She clutched Mike's arm and pulled her toward him. "Duck!"

With her head below the level of the dash, she couldn't see anything. Another bang sounded—definitely a shot—but no sound of a bullet hitting their car or breaking glass came. After a very long minute, she inched her way into an upright position once again.

Donovan crouched at the waist, hands clasping his hat, while Jacob—Jacob gestured with an old handgun.

Carly rolled the window down a few inches. If she got involved, she needed to have the big picture of what was going on.

"I tell you, I know what I saw."

The chief straightened a mite, one hand held in front of him. "Let's just talk about this, Jacob."

"Done talkin'. That thing is a menace. Got to get it."

Thing? Menace? Had a rabid squirrel or dog infiltrated their town? Surely whatever his target was didn't require a full arsenal of weapons. Two rifles rested against a gas pump, along with the pistol the older man held.

The chief tried again. "You should have called us, Jacob. We would'a come out and taken care of it."

The mechanic and last bastion of one of the founding families of the town spat on the ground. "Tried callin'. That young whippersnapper said it wasn't no emergency. You'd see to it in the mornin'."

Carly stifled a chuckle. Sounded like Officer Meyers, all right. The lad loved the forensic side of the job, but wasn't too keen to answer what he considered crank calls after hours.

Mike squeezed her hand. "What's going on?"

"I think it's safe to sit up. Jacob is shooting at a rabid dog. Or squirrel." She considered the scene before her. "I think."

Mike sat up. "You think?"

"Well, he hasn't actually come out and said. Just mentioned a

79

menace. That needed dealing with."

"Oh, that's fine then. We can go home. Nothing here for us."

She gripped his forearm. "Wait a minute. Something else is happening."

Jacob had lowered his voice so now she couldn't hear his words, but he was holding his hand about the height of a retriever from the ground. Then around four feet apart. If that's the size of the rabid animal he was shooting at, this was no squirrel or rabbit.

Then he lifted one foot and pointed to his boot.

A large dog that wore Doc Martens?

She groaned. "I think we're out here on a fool's errand."

"Wouldn't surprise me one bit. What's he saying?"

"I think he's telling the chief he saw a Labrador wearing work boots."

Mike shook his head. "I suspected Jacob of drinking away slow afternoons. But he's never gone this far before."

"He's still a brilliant mechanic. Not to mention he knows the pulse of this town."

"True. But now he might also know the pulse of the police station from the inside out, if Donovan arrests him for disturbing the peace."

Carly glanced around. Several cars hovered at the periphery of the action, and several faces peeked through upper floor apartments over the shops nearby. "Nobody seems angry or disturbed. More of a novelty, I suppose."

"Sure, until an errant bullet goes awry and shoots a hole in somebody's car, or their window. Or them."

She slapped at his arm. "Stop, Mike. I'm sure Chief Donovan won't let things get that far."

"Oh, so now you're singing his praises?"

"Not exactly, but—oh, wait, now what's going on?"

Chief Donovan dropped his hand and stepped aside, gesturing for Jacob to go ahead of him. The two crossed the street and disappeared behind the buildings, into the alleyway behind.

Carly unbuckled her seat belt and, not even waiting for Mike to open her door, stepped out. The cool breeze off the harbor, coupled with the ever-present fog rolling in from the ocean, chilled her to the bone. She should have worn something warmer.

She rounded the front of the car but Mike blocked her way. Again.

She brought up short, her nose barely reaching the second button on his shirt. She stepped to one side, but he matched her. Back again, but like a basketball guard, he held her in place.

Finally, she exhaled and peeked up at him. "What?"

His chocolate brown eyes stared down at her, warming her heart, and the dimple in his chin bespoke his European heritage. "You are not going down that alley."

"By myself."

"No, I just said—"

"You didn't finish the sentence. I am not going down that alley by myself." She ripped his hand. "So, come on. I want to see what's going on."

They trotted across the street in the steps of the police chief and the town's only mechanic. Two men vital to the well-being of the town—and their autos.

And she couldn't very well let them waltz into a dangerous situation without backup, could she?

+ + +

Mike groaned as Carly dragged him along like a puppy. What was it with this woman who simply couldn't leave well enough alone? No matter what was happening, she had to be involved.

And what was wrong with him that he couldn't stand up to her? All she had to do was bat her eyelashes at him, and he was along for the ride.

Just like tonight. Like now. He had no idea what was going on, yet here he was, ducking and slithering through an alley in the middle of the night, following two men to who knew where.

Okay, it was eight, not midnight. And he knew the two men.

Carly stopped in her tracks and pressed him against the wall.

81

"Shush."

He wouldn't point out that he hadn't uttered a word or made a sound since their arrival in this unlikely place. In fact, in all the twenty or so years he'd lived in Bear Cove, he never before found reason to be in this alley.

Yet here they were.

He leaned close to her. "Can you tell me what I'm searching for?"

"Something the size of a retriever." Her breath, coming in wheezy pants and whispers, made understanding what she said more difficult. "Wearing boots."

What? "I could have sworn you said we're chasing down a golden retriever in army boots?"

"Don't recognize the specific breed or the brand of footwear. But yes, something like that."

Well, now he knew both the chief and Jacob—and toss in Carly for good measure—were off their rockers. Carly he could attribute to whatever was going on in her head, but the chief?

He squeezed her hand twice until she looked back at him. "That makes no sense at all. Are you sure?"

"Nope. Depends on how good Jacob is at charades."

What a party game had to do with this, he couldn't fathom. He pulled her hand. "Come on. We're going back to the car, and then we're going home. I'd like to pretend this never happened."

But she resisted, planting her heels against his pull, growing roots, from the feel of it. "No. I want to stay. Please. You're here to protect me from whatever it is."

"And who will protect me?"

She chuckled. "You're my knight in shining armor, remember?"

He sighed. There was no winning this battle. "Yeah, and you're my full-time job." He quirked his chin in the direction the other two went. "Can you see them?"

"Barely." She stepped ahead then paused. "They stopped at Amanda's shop."

"And how can you tell that from this distance?"

82

"That's her pale pink dumpster."

Right. Only Amanda would insist something as utilitarian and dirty must be painted in the main palette of her shop. He recalled the divisive topic from a few years ago. Half the town wanted it to stay in the dull black of the original, and half the town—mostly the women—agreed that painting the metal container made a statement.

Amanda won when she agreed to pay for the paintwork herself and to maintain it free from graffiti. Thus far, she'd upheld her end of the bargain.

Well, at least tonight, the color served a purpose.

Carly tugged on his hand again. "Let's move closer."

They inched forward, ducking into the shadow of a doorway and holding their breath once when Donovan stared their direction, before easing out and continuing. Heart pounding, Mike would never admit aloud he was rather enjoying this little escapade. Perhaps knowing that even if they were caught, there would be no serious repercussions enabled him to experience the moment to its fullest.

Not that this would be practice for the real thing at a later date. No siree. One time and once only.

About ten feet from where the two men stood, Carly ducked behind an original black dumpster. "We should be able to hear them from here."

He raised over the edge of the container. Donovan shone a light on the ground around the rear door of Amanda's shop. He panned out in a half-circle away from the buildings, then followed something away from them in the opposite direction. Jacob, his gun at the ready, poked a stick in the pink dumpster as though expecting something to jump up at him.

Carly shifted and half stood. "I don't see anything, do you?"

"Nope."

No sooner was the word out of his mouth than a shadow separated itself from the rear of the dumpster and headed back the way they'd come. Jacob whirled and fired a shot in its direction. Mike pulled Carly down beside him, wrapping his arms around her. Another shot. Footsteps running along the alley. A strange gait. Thump. Thunk. Thump.

Thunk.

Jacob called to the chief. "This way. It went this way. Come on."

The two men pounded past where Mike cowered with Carly next to his chest. Recognizable steps. Thump. Thump. Thump. Thump.

Exactly as he'd expect.

So, what was the other sound?

He stood and gripped Carly's hand when the two rounded the exit of the alley. No point arguing for why they should simply go home. She wouldn't hear of it, and he, too, wanted to know what they'd witnessed.

At the far end of the alley, Jacob and Donovan stood, peering side to side. The old mechanic's pistol hung at his side.

When Mike and Carly approached them, Jacob whirled about, raising the weapon.

Mike's own hands shot up in surrender. "It's only us."

Jacob's shoulders relaxed and he lowered the gun. "Sorry. Thought that creature flanked us."

Carly stepped forward. "What creature? We saw nothing."

Mike bit his tongue. No, she likely didn't see that shadow racing down the alley. Probably didn't hear the strange footsteps generated by its rapid exit.

But he had.

"What I was tryin' to explain to this man here." Jacob gestured to the chief using his pistol. "I saw a strange monster from the window in my garage. Stood on two legs, it did. 'Bout this high." He held his palm flat to the ground about three feet up. "And we saw its prints. Over there in the dirt. And near the door."

Carly stiffened beside him, then she chuckled. "Probably was a dog, Jacob. But you mentioned rabies? That's more serious."

"Snarled at me when I went after it. That's why I went for my guns. And shot at it." He shook his head. "Not a dog, neither. Only two legs. And one wearing a boot. The other like a cow or something."

"A goat."

Mike stared at his wife, unsure whether she'd spoken the words aloud, or merely thought them.

84

Aloud, he decided, judging by Jacob and Donovan's reaction.

The old man nodded.

And the chief laughed. "You can't tell me you seriously believe this, do you?"

Carly's shoulders slumped. "That's the second time this week I heard about such a creature being sighted." She lifted her chin. "And if it's true, trouble is ahead. It already killed at least one man that we know of."

+ + +

Carly's shoulders slumped as she and Mike drove back along Main Street, taking the long way toward home and bed. Thinking about her cozy house, with the lights left on and a hot cup of tea warmed her up a tad.

Or was it her imagination?

She shrugged deeper into her thin jacket as the fog swirled low on the ground all around their car. The heater blowing hot air into the cabin made little difference. What was it with harbor towns that attracted the low-lying cloudlike vapor as soon as the sun went down? Something to do with the difference between the air and water temperatures, most likely.

She clutched Mike's hand and edged as close to him as she could given the console between them. Her head ached, her muscles screamed for rest, and her vision dimmed—a function of age, MS, exhaustion, the fog—or all of the above? She didn't know, and frankly, she didn't want to know tonight. She glanced over at him. "I'm glad you're driving tonight. I can't see a foot in front of—"

A form materialized out of the vapor, and Carly gasped.

She stared in the object's direction and yanked on Mike's hand. Keeping her voice low, she lamented she had no weapon. "Mike."

Her hoarse whisper sounded like she'd shouted through a PA system at a homecoming football game.

Mike turned to face her. "What?"

She pointed toward the approaching figure. "There."

He slowed the car, easing over to the side of the road, and turned off the engine. "Maybe someone needs help."

"Or maybe we should keep going and mind our own business."

"Not very neighborly." He switched the wipers on to clear the

85

condensation from the windshield, then rolled down his window. "Amanda. What are you doing out here tonight?"

The shop owner's disheveled hair, misbuttoned coat, and mismatched footwear—a yellow ducky boot and a red penny loafer—screamed volumes about the woman's state of mind. "Finally. I found somebody." She stepped up to the driver's window and gripped the door, knuckles white. "I'm so scared."

Carly leaned across the seat. "What's going on? Why are you out here, wandering the streets at night? Alone?"

"I tried to contact the police department, but I kept getting voice mail. Apparently they're already out on another call."

Mike nodded. "Yes, we just came from downtown."

Amanda peered at first Mike then Carly. "Why were you involved?"

Carly smiled up at her. Maybe she could set the woman at ease. "We heard the gunshots, saw the lights. Went down to see what was going on."

Amanda glanced toward downtown. "And what was it about? And what could be so important that nobody remained in the police station to answer other citizen's emergencies?"

Carly straightened. "You had an emergency?"

"That's what I said. Why else would I be calling the police?"

"What was it?"

"My house was broken into."

Carly sighed. She wouldn't be crawling into her bed anytime soon by the looks of it.

+ + +

There. A bandage and a dash of whiskey to staunch the flow of blood from the graze. That idiot's last shot came too close for comfort. Yet another reason to finish the assignment and leave this inbred town. In Peru, a private citizen would never be permitted to fire—or even own—a firearm without strict background checks and training. Yet that idiot of a mechanic waved his gun around like a flag at a parade. Shooting at shadows.

Fools, so easily led astray by an old wives tale. Monsters conjured from the legends of the past and by drunken visions. And because the stories were passed down orally through generations and at last found their way onto the information highway, they must be true.

Such distractions would be used for a good cause, to keep the weak in their place, and to ensure that the organization's goals were accomplished.

For that, any fairy tale would do.

People were so gullible.

Chapter 9

When the telephone rang later that night, Carly groaned. Her head ached, and her body protested when she so much as wriggled a toe. Was this what life would be like from now on? Pain, pain, and more pain?

Mike passed her the handset. "It's Amanda. I told her you didn't want to be disturbed, but she insisted."

"Yes, she can be very persuasive." Carly pressed the phone to her ear after checking the time. At least it was still Friday. Barely. "Amanda, what can I do for you?"

She resisted adding *this time*. After spending two hours with the woman while she answered endless questions about how she knew her home was burgled—no forced entry, nothing missing that she could tell—and rolling her eyes each time Amanda insisted she simply *knew*.

However, given the other strange happenings—in Bear Cove and in Peru—Carly wasn't ready to discount this as another of Amanda's imaginings.

"Hope I didn't wake you."

"No, I had to get up to answer the phone. Why are you calling me at twenty minutes before midnight? Are you in a different time zone and don't know the time here? If so, you must have traveled fast, since I last saw you less than two hours ago. I hope you're somewhere fun, although you could have sent an email. Or a postcard."

"It's about the monster."

Not again. Or rather, not still. She and Mike tacitly agreed not to mention anything to Amanda about *El Chullachaqui* or Jacob Roy's assertions of what he saw that evening. And the chief found no strange footprints outside or inside the woman's home. Seemed news spread fast that something was on the loose in town. In a few hours, apparently. And with Jacob Roy sworn to secrecy—a man who kept his word, by the way—the only other source besides her and Mike was the police chief.

And she suspected he'd sooner have his tongue cut out than leak this news to anybody.

Carly sighed. "Monster?"

"Yes. Residents spotted it around town, you know."

Ah, more than a simple rumor. "Really?"

"Yes. And there are footprints."

"Who told you this?"

"That nice young Officer Adam."

Now the shop owner was on a first name basis with the young man. Interesting. "And he told you what?"

"That Jacob Roy shot up the whole downtown tonight. That a posse chased the monster into the alley."

"Did they get it?"

"No. It slipped past them and escaped. But they saw footprints near the door of my shop."

"I'm sure there are plenty of footprints down that alley. The trash man. Kids on a shortcut. The odd drunk passed out in a doorway."

"I'll have you know that no inebriated person left these marks. I saw them for myself."

This was news. Carly switched the handset to the other ear. "You did?"

"Well, not literally. Officer Adam emailed me a picture the chief took. And the prints are exactly what Rogelio described. One boot, one goat."

"But nobody actually saw the creature?"

"No. Although Jacob thought maybe he winged it."

"It has wings, too?"

"A figure of speech, Carly. That's all. And they saw some blood

90

drops in the area."

Another tidbit. "Well, thanks for the information. See you tomorrow. In the daylight."

"I'm scared, Carly. Alone here in this house. Alone in the shop day after day."

Interesting. That contradicted her carloads of customers story. "Maybe you should stay in your shop, then. You could ask the chief to make sure an officer checks in with you every hour."

A sobbing gasp. "You mean I could lay in my own blood, murdered, for an hour before somebody found me? I don't think so."

"Well, I don't know what to tell you, Amanda."

"Don't you have an extra en-suite where I could stay for a few days?"

She hadn't shared her medical concerns with Amanda and had no intention of doing so now. Not until she had her final answer. And absolutely not before she told her kids. She nudged Mike and made a choking motion, her hand to her throat. Thankfully, he took the hint and emitted a strangled, rasping cough.

"Hang on, Amanda. Mike hasn't been feeling well." She waited five seconds before continuing. "Might be flu."

"Oh. Well, I don't want to catch that, for sure. Never mind, I'll come up with something else."

"Maybe a friend would stay with you?"

"Oh, I won't put anybody in danger."

Nice. But it's okay to lure the killer to our house.

She pasted on a smile. "Understood."

"I'll email you the picture of the prints so you can get started on that first thing."

Carly glanced at the clock. News alert: it already *was* first thing in the morning. Not that she had any intention of beginning work now. Besides which, she'd already seen the footprints first hand and up close.

No doubt about it, her friend was creeped out. And with good cause.

+ + +

Listening at windows is becoming a necessary part of this job. Still, it is amazing how much information people reveal when they don't know they are being overheard. Priceless details.

The creation of the footprints was ingenious. Something learned years ago but never applied until now. Surprising sometimes how technology was worthless, and old-fashioned ingenuity was key.

Chapter 10

Sitting at her desk on Saturday morning, Carly fought against a rising tide of nausea and vertigo, no doubt caused by the pounding headache behind her eyes. Or the knot in the muscles below her shoulders. Or by the patience demanded of her as she awaited the results of the MRI.

Or all three.

Kind of like her life right now. Hurry up and wait had become her new mantra.

She shook her head at her foolish thoughts as she addressed the paperwork mess that somehow blossomed in the past few days. Unlike her husband's vertical filing system, she much preferred order. Paper, in a file folder in a cabinet drawer. Digital, in a folder in email or on her hard drive. Easy to find using the SEARCH tool.

She glanced across the expanse of their back-to-back desks and smiled at Mike. He always seemed to find what he searched for, no matter how disorganized the papers appeared. And he was one of those people who believed an email was best retrieved if left in the Inbox, and a digital file easiest found on his desktop.

She rubbed at her left temple. Maybe she should lie down. Or have a cup of tea. Or both.

Or maybe now was the time for The Talk. The one they'd both been avoiding for the past few days. Maybe even the past few years. "Mike, can we talk for a minute, or are you deep into something?"

He turned from his computer and faced her. "Nothing that can't wait. What's up?"

Studying his boyishly handsome face raised something else in her. Not caused by anything physical. No, this was a ham-sized dollop of love for this man, who'd stood by her through thick and thin for the past twenty years. Who'd stood by his first wife through her illness until she passed away, leaving him the sole parent to two young adult children.

Would he have to go through all that again?

Perhaps she should continue agreeing not to speak about tough topics.

No, that wasn't fair. To either of them.

She drew a deep breath then exhaled. "I want to talk about Monday, and then the short term and long-term decisions we might have to make."

He sat back in his chair and folded his arms over his chest. "I don't see any purpose in making those kinds of decisions when we don't know what's going on." He leaned forward, elbows on the desk, a frown marring his brow. "I mean, could be a sinus infection. Or something else minor, like that."

She peered at him, holding his gaze. "Do you really think it is?"

He stayed still a long moment. She counted her pounding heartbeat in her ears. Four. Five. Six. Seven.

Then he shook his head. "No, I guess I don't." He reached across the desk, and she slipped her hand into his. "I love you so much. I wish it could be me instead of you going through this."

She offered him a half-smile. "I'm glad it's me. You're the stronger one. You can carry on easier without me than I could without you."

He snatched his hand back as though she'd burned him. "Don't say that. You. Are. Not. Going. To. Die."

"Even if it's the worst thing, MS, you're right. At least, not for a long time, hopefully. But we will have to make changes."

He sat back, shoulders slumped. "I know. And we probably should have talked about this long ago. But you know how I am."

Now she landed a full smile. "Yes, I do. Always optimistic that

94

things will work out for the best. And it always has. No matter what I've thrown at you, you catch it and hand it off like a pro." She shook her head. "I don't know how you do it."

"Like I've told you before. If you can't change it, run with it."

She sighed. "An axiom I've never subscribed to myself, as you know."

"Because of the word *run*. I know. Never waste a heartbeat."

She frowned. "Maybe I should've exercised more. Do you think that would have kept me from this?"

Mike spread his hands wide on the desk. "We don't even know what *it* is yet. Let's talk about what we do know."

"Okay. Something is happening to me physically. Concerned Doc Walsh enough to order an MRI and blood work."

"Right. And he wouldn't do that unless he thought something was up. We can accept that as fact." Mike toyed with his now-lukewarm coffee. "What's our next step?" He held up a hand when she opened her mouth to speak. "Based on what we know."

That was a tough question, because her mind was already moving in several directions at once, coming up with various scenarios based on what they might learn on Monday. Then she sat forward. "We're at an age where things are changing. Our physical bodies aren't as resilient as they once were. Our mental capabilities aren't as vast as they used to be. And our emotional aspects can't keep us firing on all eight cylinders when either the physical or mental fails us."

He nodded. "So, what you're saying is we need to make some changes. Small ones at first, maybe, until we arrive at our ultimate goal."

"Which is what, exactly?"

He pulled a notepad toward him. "If money were no object, and time didn't matter, what do you want to accomplish with the forty or so years you have left?"

She wished she had that long. Then again, if Doc Walsh was over-enthusiastic with his diagnosis, maybe she could. "I'd want to spend more time with the kids and grands."

He jotted a note. "It would be nice to travel more. Not related to

95

work."

She nodded. "Me, too. I'd like to ease out of work gracefully, not waiting until I fell flat on my face."

Another note. "Make that another me-too."

"Do you have any projects you'd like to get done? Around the house, maybe?"

He chuckled. "I can see it now. A honey-do list as long as my arm."

Now she laughed. "Sorry, that was the list for last year. Added to the lists from previous years, it's now about two stories tall."

"Seriously?" He tossed the pen on the paper. "Sounds like you've already mapped out my retirement for me."

"Not at all. We have some things coming up in our more immediate time, however."

He pulled out his pocket planner. "Got the doctor's appointment here for Tuesday afternoon. What else?"

"Church on Sunday."

"Right." He wrote in the small booklet. "What time?"

She turned to her computer and typed in the church's name then scanned the page. "Eleven." She glanced at him over the screen. "Victoria said they have a potluck this Sunday following the service, and she invited us. As guests, we don't need to bring anything."

"Sounds like a deal. Feed the soul and then feed the body. My kind of church."

She giggled. "Mike, you don't go to church only for the food."

"Maybe not, but it's an impressive way to lure folks in."

"Now you're making it sound like a trap. Or a spider web." She shivered. She hated spiders. And wasps. Creepy-crawlies of most kinds, in fact. Not earthworms, though. They moved slow, didn't bite or sting, and helped her garden grow. "A garden."

"What about a garden? You have lots of flowers already."

"Maybe we could learn to plant vegetables. A couple of fruit trees. Can our own food."

He shook his head. "Next you'll have us installing a wood stove and getting off the grid."

Now it was her turn to fold her arms. And she added a mock glare for emphasis. "You're mocking me. But I spend a lot of time and money at the farmer's market in the summer. I thought this was something we could do together."

"I was teasing. Anything else?"

"Add something just for you."

"Haven't given it much thought."

She pursed her lips. "What about that photography course you've talked about for years?"

"Guess if I really wanted to do it, I'd'a done it by now."

"But in semi-retirement, you'd have more time."

"True. I'll add it to the list so we keep it in mind." He wrote on the paper. "What about us taking a course together?"

"Oh, like what?"

"I don't know." He sat back again and tapped the pencil against his chin. That strong mandible with the darling dimple. "Bird watching? You enjoyed the ramble we went on with Jacob Roy last fall."

"Yes, I did. Might be something to add on our bucket list." She stared at a dust web in the corner of her office. How had she not noticed that before? "Wonder how Jacob is doing? He appeared scared after his run-in with whatever he thought he saw."

"Oh, he saw something. Remember the footprints Amanda told you about?"

She drew her focus back to him. "You don't really think the jungle monster came all the way from Peru searching for jewelry, do you?"

"Don't know. But something left those tracks. And he saw something more than a shadow that night. And where there's smoke, there's fire, I always say."

She chuckled. Wow, three times in one day. Felt good. "I've never heard you say that before, Mike Turnquist. But I will agree with you. Something's going on. And I will understand it, if it's the last thing I do."

As soon as the words left her mouth, a chill ran up her spine. Then down. Leaving her hair bristling and her skin cold and clammy.

97

She hoped solving Amanda's mystery wouldn't be the last entry in her diary of life.

+ + +

Carly's cell phone rang, and she rolled her eyes before setting down her mystery novel. Seemed she never sat for more than a few minutes in the sunroom before an interruption tramped through her relaxation time. Apparently even Saturday afternoons weren't secure from such intrusions.

Hopefully, not Amanda again.

She glanced at CALLER ID. Chief Donovan. "Hello?"

"Didn't interrupt anything, did I?"

She resisted the urge to sigh. "Nothing more important than a great cozy I've been reading."

"Cozy? I know about tea cozies from my grandmother. But a book?"

"Yeah. Think Agatha Christie or Jessica Fletcher." She stretched her legs out to catch the last of the afternoon sun. "What's up?"

"Wanted to let you know somebody broke into the PD last night."

"Surely you're joking. Who would break into a cop shop?"

"Interesting question. And when I have the answer, I'll let you know."

"And you're telling me this because?"

"I know you've been working with Amanda about this Peru connection, and we think this break-in might be related to that case."

She sat up straight and planted her feet flat on the floor. "I wouldn't call it a case, Chief. I'm not even sure there is really a Peru connection at all. She likely just blew everything out of proportion."

"I hear what you're saying. And what you're not. She can be melodramatic, to be sure." His office chair squeaked, and Carly imagined him landing his foot on the corner of his desk. "Still, she had a break-in at her shop."

"So, getting back to your call, was anything taken?"

"No, that's the strange thing. The criminal broke into the evidence locker and searched through the boxes of evidence we collected at Amanda's shop and home. Not that we had much from her house,

98

because she didn't see anybody. Or at least, nobody she could describe or identify. A couple of smudged footprints that could have been there an hour or a month. A broken twig on her rose bush that, again, could be new or not."

"Footprints? Where?"

"In the plant bed near a window. But like I said—"

"Not likely it was there very long, Chief. We had a torrential downpour last week that would have washed away anything legible."

His chair squealed again and a thunk! indicated he'd sat up straight. "Right. I forgot that."

Carly's mind raced through the list of possibilities. Amanda might have been correct. Maybe she saw somebody at her house last night. But if so, what were they searching for in the police department? And if she was imagining things, how might this break-in be connected?

"Chief, if nothing was taken, then what they were seeking for mustn't have been there. But what could that be?"

"That's one scenario. Another is they wanted to see what we had, maybe because there is a piece of evidence that would point to them. But if we don't have it, they might relax and make a mistake, in which case we'll catch them."

"That would be nice. I'm sure it would set Amanda's mind at rest."

"And Jacob Roy's, too. He's a tough old coot, though. Saw him today working at his garage like nothing ever happened."

Carly chuckled. "It would be nice to get through one night without something going on. No doubt about it. It sure feels like an epidemic of weirdness is going through town."

The chief nodded. "More than usual, you mean."

"You said it, I didn't." She peered out into the backyard, where a squirrel raced up and down a tree on this warm February afternoon. "Was there any forced entry at the station?"

"Interesting you should ask. No, there wasn't. Which is why we didn't realize until an hour or so ago. Officer Meyers went into the room to place a piece of evidence from another case, and that's when he saw several boxes out of place."

Carly's ears perked up. "Another case? A veritable crime wave."

"Nothing important. A stolen car. Likely kids out joyriding. Still waiting on latents to come back, but the owner reported the car missing in Bangor two weeks ago."

Interesting. A stolen car found abandoned in town. "Why would kids steal a car in the big city then leave it here? Did they steal another? Or did they take the bus home?"

"Good question. You don't think there's any connection to this Peru thing, do you?"

"Dunno. But we might keep an eye out for a stranger on foot. If he lost his ride—wait a minute. Where did you find the car?"

"Abandoned at the far end of Main Street. Parked there for the past three days. Mrs. Olsen at the pharmacy called it in."

"So, if it wasn't kids, then whoever stole it must have stolen another to replace it. Or bought a car. Or had an accomplice arrive from elsewhere."

Chief Donovan sighed. "Sounds like you're making more work for me. I was going to report it to Bangor PD and let them send a tow truck for it. Next I'll ask around town for heisted vehicles. And recently purchased cars. And another stranger in town."

"Ask at the motel up on the highway. Our perp would find it easier to stay hidden if he didn't hang around in public too much."

Donovan chuckled again. "Listen to you. Perp. Talkin' like a real cop."

"I sense an insult close on the tail of that statement. Sounds like the perfect time for me to say goodbye."

"Talk to you later, Carly. Thanks for the information."

"Any time, Chief. Any time."

She disconnected the call and set the phone on the table near her elbow. Her novel screamed for her to pick it up and continue.

Instead, she focused on the leafless rose bush outside the door. A broken twig on one of her plants might not garner attention because she didn't prune and baby her garden. However, Amanda was different.

Everything perfectly manicured and trimmed. The soil raked. Leaves picked up. Flowering plants dead headed. All the time.

If Amanda says there were footprints or a twig out of place, Carly would bet her last dollar both were recent.

+ + +

That persnickety woman will be the downfall of the mission. And perhaps the organization. Not the nosey accountant lady. The one who stole what belonged to the country.

There was no way to know she had such a green thumb and would notice footprints or that tiny broken branch on the prickly thorn bush. The one that tore a hole in a favorite pair of pants. Which now went into the trash because the clothing could prove incriminating.

Circumstantial, yes, but still. I could take no chances with this mission. Success was so close at hand. Failure was not an option.

But breaking into the police department—that was delightful. A fitting ending to an otherwise frustrating day. Unfortunately, what I sought wasn't there. Which was just as well.

Like in the alley the other night. No, that was foolishness. A better plan would have been to wait until the old man left for the night. He always closed up by ten. Surveillance of the garage proved that. And how could I know he had a gun? Weren't Downeast'ers supposed to be peace loving?

And now that they found the car, other arrangements needed making. Buy one? That would require registration with the state. Steal another? The police would be on high alert with the discovery of the first. Left few options.

But one would come to mind.

One always did.

Chapter 11

Carly waved to Jacob Roy as she turned the corner onto Main Street on Saturday morning. "Hi, Jacob. What's new?"

"Not much, Miss Carly. Not much." The older man swiped his hands in a greasy rag which he then stuffed into the chest pocket of his overalls. "And with you?"

"Same old, same old."

"Ayuh."

His usually infectious smile seemed a tad off today. As though he hadn't slept well. But his quintessential Downeast'er response cheered her. Probably her imagination, wanting to make a mystery out of a molehill.

She slowed her pace then paused. "Quiet downtown last night?"

"Ayuh." He exhaled, shoulders drooping. "Best get back to it."

No doubt about it. Something was amiss. Or afoot, as Sherlock Holmes would say.

And Mike often enough accused her of being the 20th Century version of the detective, minus the meerschaum pipe and deerstalker hat and cape, that is.

"Got time for a coffee, Jacob?"

He glanced up and down the street as though checking for incoming customers, then tossed her a smile. "That I do, Miss Carly. That I do."

She waved him across the street. "I'm headed for the Dew Drop

Inn. Treat's on me."

While not exactly the entire truth, her invitation to her old friend was close enough. Since losing his wife more than ten years before, he often seemed in a world of his own. And lately, his clothing was a little more unkempt, and she noted he'd missed the same spot shaving for several days in a row now, judging by the length of the hair peeking out from under his jawline.

Still, he appeared healthy enough for a man of his age. Whatever that was. He didn't stoop, and he turned up to work at his family-owned garage every day. He was the last of his family, as he and Ethel never had children. His one claim to fame was his great-great-grandfather was one of the founding fathers of the town.

He worked a toothpick from one side of his mouth to the other without laying a finger on it. A lifelong habit, she suspected.

"Jacob, what you going to have?"

She held open the door for him, waving him in ahead of her.

Instead, he shook his head and gripped the edge of the door, knobby knuckles and age-spotted hands still strong. "Ladies first."

She curtsied. "Don't know how much of a lady I am, but thank you."

She stepped inside, nodding to Victoria behind the counter, and after a quick survey of the area, headed for a booth in a corner.

But Jacob stopped her with a touch on her arm. "Let's sit here at a table in the window. So's I can keep an eye on the station. In case anybody needs gas, you know."

Mid-morning in Bear Cove was probably the least busy time of the day, but Carly nodded and changed direction toward an empty chrome table with red vinyl-covered chairs. Jacob pulled out her seat for her, and she slid onto the cold surface and picked up a menu waiting on the table.

She perused the diner's offerings, although she practically knew them by heart. When Victoria offered coffee, she nodded. "Thanks. What's good today?"

As expected, the waitress planted her fists on her ample hips.

104

"Girl, everythin' is good here. All. The. Time." She filled Jacob's cup without asking then set the pot on the table. "What'cha want this mornin', Jacob?"

"Whatever you want to fix for me." He chuckled. "That's what I said to my sweet Ethel whenever she asked me what I wanted to eat." He stared out the window. "She was a wonderful cook."

"Don't I know that." Victoria's voice broke. "Taught me everything I know."

Jacob brightened, and he returned to present company. "That she did. And don't you forget it."

Carly smiled at the familiar banter between the two. A well-rehearsed bit that never grew old. For either of them. "Then I'll have whatever you want to make for me, too."

Victoria's brow pulled down. "Now listen here. He's the only one can order like that. You decide for yourself."

Oops. Would she never be a full-fledged member of the town? Over twenty years living here, and she still didn't understand the social dynamics. "Then I'll have what he's having."

Victoria's face relaxed, and she nodded. "Quick thinkin', Miss Carly. Two specials it is. Coming right up."

Carly leaned across the table. "Any idea what we're getting?"

He shook his head. "Nope. It's different every time." He sipped his coffee. "Oh, that's good."

Carly agreed. Victoria made the best restaurant coffee she'd ever tasted. Never weak, never bitter. Always perfect taste and temperature. "No more sightings?"

He glanced left and right as though afraid somebody might listen in. Apparently satisfied, he shook his head. "Nope. But you believe I saw something?"

"Absolutely. Something. Or somebody. I'm not sure what they're up to. Has the chief said anything else?"

"Nope. But something spooked Miss Amanda. She won't go down that alley anymore. Goes in through the front door. Has Mavis's son taking out her trash for her. And I hear she's thinking of painting that

105

dumpster black again. Doesn't want to draw attention to her store that way."

"You've talked to her?"

"Ayuh. She gets her gas here. And her car serviced, too. In fact, this morning." His eyes widened. "'Spect you haven't heard, have you?"

"About what?" Couldn't she go one day without another mystery? "Something to do with Amanda?"

"Fact. She's in the hospital." He sat back, arms over his chest. "Called on her newfangled cell phone thing." He scratched his neck. "Not sure I think those contraptions are good, mind you. I don't cotton to them meself. I like the old-fashioned Ma Bell kind of phone."

Carly's under-caffeinated brain struggled to untangle the older man's stream-of-consciousness conversation. "What?"

He leaned across the table and raised his voice a notch. "I said—"

She laid a hand on his. "I heard you. But what were you saying about her being in the hospital?"

"Sure enough." He relaxed again as Victoria set two plates on the table. "Looks good. Thank you."

Carly picked up her fork, mesmerized by the mountain of hash browns, the sausage, and the stuffed omelet before her. Not to mention the six slices of homemade bread. And homemade jelly. She groaned. If she ate like this every day, she'd be big as a house.

Jacob cleared his throat, and she met his gaze. "I like to give thanks for my food."

Heat rushed to her cheeks as she set the fork aside and closed her eyes. Seemed every time she turned around, God was hitting her over the head.

After a quick prayer, Jacob dug into his food like he hadn't eaten in a week. Carly followed suit—albeit more sedately. No doubt about it, today's special was delish.

By the time they'd polished off their food, Jacob seemed more in the mood to talk. "Like I said, I called because her car was due for a check-up. No answer at her home, so I tried her cell phone. Wasn't sure my old dialer would connect with hers, but it sure did."

106

"A phone by any other name is still a phone."

She thought her paraphrase witty and à propos, but Jacob's frown told her he didn't get it. "Huh? Never mind. Anyway, she went into the community hospital last night because she got sick. They think it's some kind of food poisoning."

"What do you mean?"

He shrugged. "Just that. She thinks she ate something that made her sick."

"Does she know what?"

"Nope. She said she was feeling fine until she went home and made dinner. Ask her about it." He drained his coffee cup. "All's I know is she didn't want to schedule her maintenance check until she was back on her feet."

Apparently Jacob took this incident as a personal affront. Hoping to release some of the mechanic's tension, she tossed him a half-smile. "I enjoyed spending a little time with you. We should do this more often."

"Been a long time since we chatted, for sure. I don't want to make your husband jealous."

Carly chuckled. Another longstanding joke. "Oh, he knows you would never act unbecomingly."

"Good. He's right. I'm a married man, after all."

She stood and set several bills on the table for their meal. "Yes, you are."

Jacob held the door for her exit, and they ambled to the corner. He tipped his head and headed back to his garage. Carly waited until he crossed the street, even though traffic was nil, before heading back toward her original destination: the alley leading to the back door of Amanda's shop. As she did, she dialed the woman's cell.

She passed the bank, Sweet Tooth Bakery, the Snip'n Clip, slowing at the rear entrance of the Dew Drop Inn. However, when nobody came out, she carried on, past the used book store, the thrift and consignment shop, and the real estate office, now boarded up, where Susan used to work.

Arriving at Amanda's shop, she hesitated. How many rings was that? Six? Seven? Shouldn't the woman's voice mail have kicked in by—

"Hello?"

"Amanda? Is that you?"

"Carly? Who else would it be? You called me, didn't you?"

"I did. But it rang so many times—"

"I was in the bathroom. At the hospital. I got food poisoning."

"I know."

"How?" A groan. "Is it all around town already?"

"I don't think so. Victoria didn't mention it."

Another groan. More like a moan-groan this time. "You talked to her about it?"

"No." Carly checked the ground around the door. No prints she could see. She strolled over to the dumpster and peered over the edge. Nothing moving in there, either. Thankfully. "Jacob told me."

A long sigh. "Leave it to him to blab it all over town. I'll never live this down."

What was the woman talking about? "Nothing to be ashamed about getting food poisoning. Happens to the best of us."

A sniff. Carly pictured the woman with her nose in the air, peering down her proboscis at her. "Might happen to you, but not to me. I am most fastidious in my food storage and preparation."

"So, what went wrong?"

A squawk. "Why assume something went wrong? Sounds like you think I made myself sick."

Carly peered around the back of the dumpster. Nothing back here, either, except a nasty-looking puddle of something that resembled like vomit. Oh, Amanda would not be happy to see that.

Maybe she should take a picture with her phone and send it to her.

T'would serve her right.

Carly exhaled. The woman was sick. Likely up all night getting her stomach pumped. Or something equally disgusting. "Not at all. What did you eat?"

"A salad from the diner for lunch. Sweet tea. Then I went back to

108

the shop. Unpacked some items. An hour later, dizzy, cold sweats, and—well, vomiting."

Carly smiled at her friend's reluctance to describe her body's reaction to a bad mushroom. "What do you think was off?"

"Nothing. If I suspected that, I wouldn't have eaten it. I am not an idiot."

No, but her tone implied Carly was. She gritted her teeth. "What do the doctors say?"

"Not much. But I will get to the bottom of this."

"I'd better let you go so you can rest."

"Thanks for calling. And please don't tell anybody."

"No worries."

Strange. For a woman who insisted she did nothing to bring on this bout of food poisoning, Amanda was certainly insistent nobody else know.

Did the woman protest too much?

And if so, why would she poison herself?

Or perhaps she wasn't telling Carly—and perhaps the doctors, too—the truth.

And if not, what was going on?

+ + +

After leaving the alley, Carly headed for her second stop of the morning: the pharmacy.

Ever since the pregnancy test scare—although, being pregnant might be less fearsome than the possible other diagnoses facing her—she'd wanted to let Mrs. Olsen know the results.

As she passed the town hall, which housed the police and fire departments, in addition to the town clerk and mayor, Chief Donovan emerged from his car. "Hi Carly."

"Hi, Chief."

"Out for a stroll?"

She glanced back toward Amanda's shop. "Sort of. Just had breakfast with Jacob."

The chief leaned against the railing leading up to the front entry of the building. "How is he doing after his scare?"

"Seems fine. Chatty as usual."

Donovan chuckled. "Getting more than four words out of him would be a stretch."

"It's the Downeast way, Chief." She eyed the street. No vehicles moving, several pedestrians. "Business slow? Apart from the monster and Amanda's break-ins, I mean."

"You knew she's in hospital, right?" He exhaled and shifted his weight to his other foot. "Thinks some madman from South America is trying to poison her. Insists somebody is watching her house."

"Yeah, she called. Just got off the phone with her. But she didn't mention it was intentional."

Or had she? Perhaps Amanda's theatrics were more out of fear than of wanting to be the center of attention.

Maybe she should listen for the meaning behind the words, rather than simply the words themselves.

The police chief checked in both directions then sidled closer. "Had a couple of strange reports from yesterday and last night."

"How so?"

"Mrs. Olsen called and said the man who drives her supply truck claimed two boxes of crackers and some snacks were missing."

"Kids?"

He shook his head. "Don't know. It wasn't like the thief took all he had on board. More like a snatch-and-grab. Crime of convenience, as we say."

"So, either kids or somebody who needed food but didn't have the money to buy it?"

He shrugged. "Or didn't want to be seen buying it."

"Interesting. What else?"

"Clothes was missing off a clothes line five houses up from Amanda's."

"Men's or women's?"

"Men's, but could be for either, I guess. Jeans, a shirt."

"So, we still don't know if we're looking for a male or a female?"

110

He shook his head again. "Nope. And the footprints don't tell us much. Size 8 men's. But from what I've read, Peruvian men tend to be of a smaller build, so it could be a man. Or a woman with larger feet."

"And nobody saw anything?"

"No. Of course not. Or I suspect they'd have stepped in." He crossed his arms over his chest. "Somebody could have gotten hurt."

An idea blossomed. "No reports of stolen vehicles by any chance?"

"No, thank goodness. Still, regarding Bear Cove, I guess we're in the middle of a crime wave." He sighed. "Better get to work before a concerned citizen accuses me of wasting taxpayer money."

"Call me if you hear of any missing cars, will you?"

"Clothes, cars—what next?"

"Hopefully, nothing."

She waved as she continued on her way. Inside the shop, Mrs. Olsen stocked a shelf behind the glass-topped counter.

The older woman turned and smiled. "Hello. Good to see you again, dear."

"Thanks. Just wanted to let you know the test was negative."

Mrs. Olsen's smile slipped. "And how do you feel about that?"

"I'm not sure right now." Carly peered at the items in the display case. Bobby pins, hairnets, shower caps, and plastic rollers. Straight out of the sixties. She squinted. "Not being pregnant means something else is going on. So, I went to the doctor. Still waiting for the results of tests."

The shopkeeper laid her hand on Carly's. "Oh, dear. I'm sorry to hear that. Still, not knowing can be worse than knowing." A half-smile relaxed her mouth. "It was that way when Mr. Olsen got sick. We were sure it was cancer. But it wasn't. Which gave us more years together."

The woman's husband passed away fter Carly moved to town. "What was it?"

"Sarcoidosis. Affects the respiratory system. But we sure thought it was lung cancer. Even though he never smoked a single cigarette in his life. But instead we had another ten years. Praise God."

"Sounds strange to thank God when he still died."

Mrs. Olsen squeezed her hand. "Don't you see? It was a wake-up call for us. We went back to church. Grew closer in our relationship with each other and with God. Praised Him for what He was doing in our lives. Saw our two sons and their families do the same. And we enjoyed the years we had. Once he finished his treatments, he had his strength back. And his enthusiasm. And now he had a purpose. To tell everybody about Jesus." She leaned closer as though sharing a confidence. "Maybe God is trying to get your attention."

Was that possible? That God would care enough about her to even want her attention?

And what kind of god made people sick simply so He could scare them into—into what? No way did she want a relationship of any kind with a god like that.

She withdrew her hand. "Well, I wanted to let you know about the test."

"Maybe we'll see you at church?"

Carly smiled. "We'll see."

Today was an outstanding day. No dizziness. No brain fog. Maybe she'd overreacted by seeing the doctor. Most likely he'd tell her the tests were negative. Suggest she take more vitamins. Eat more greens. Exercise.

As she left the store, she chuckled. Sounded like hell on earth.

+ + +

This woman was one crazy *Americano*. First the alley, then checking the trash as if expecting *El Chullachaqui* to jump out in front of her. And what was it with appeasing the old man by buying him breakfast? What was the word? An old coot.

But following her was brilliant, even though sneaking around cars in the parking lot was not the usual method employed. Still, hearing her conversation with the cop provided useful information. No stolen cars. Of course not. No point in repeating the same mistake. Still, the missing food and money—so much prosperity in this country, and still they notice those minor items. *Estupido*—keep a low profile.

Grrr. Must be more careful. The plan must not fail.

Now on to the next step.

112

Chapter 12

When she stepped inside her house, Mike met her in the foyer. "Where have you been? I thought you said a short walk."

She stretched up on her toes and planted a kiss on his mouth. Then she patted her pocket. "I had my phone with me. If I had trouble, I'd have called."

He sniffed. "You smell like hash browns and sausage."

She rubbed her tummy. "Ran into Jacob. Took him for breakfast."

He rolled his eyes. "While I'm home by myself and starving to death?"

"You could have made yourself something."

"Nothing as good as Victoria's breakfast specials. Which one did you have?"

She lifted one shoulder in a half-shrug. "Don't know. I got what Jacob ordered. Victoria was a little miffed, but I think she got over it." She led the way to their shared office. "Going to contact Rogelio and see what's new on his end."

"What else is new in town?"

She paused and faced him halfway down the hallway. "What makes you think there is?"

"Your cheeks are flushed and you're smiling."

"Must be fresh air and exercise."

He laid the back of his hand against her forehead. "Oh-oh."

She stepped out of reach. "What's that about?"

"When I hear those words from your mouth, you either have a fever. Or you're holding something back."

She slid into her chair and turned on her computer. "There was some news." She filled him in on Amanda's food poisoning and her chat with the chief. "A veritable crime wave has hit town." She clicked onto FaceLink and selected Rogelio's account. "The good news is I've been feeling much better today."

He leaned back in his chair, hands clasped behind his head. "That is delightful."

"I mentioned it to Mrs. Olsen, and she seemed to think maybe God was behind my symptoms."

"God?" Mike sat up straight, his brow pulled down. "Why?"

A full shrug this time. "Something about getting my attention." Rogelio appeared on her screen, and she raised a forefinger to Mike to indicate she'd get back to him. "Hi, Rogelio."

"Miss Carly." He spoke to someone off-screen. "Carmen says to say hello. How are you?"

His pronunciation *jou* tickled her, reminding her that not all letters sounded the same in other languages. Take the *y* in Spanish, for example, pronounced as *j*.

"Doing well. Do you have an update for me?"

The Peruvian man's smile evaporated. "*Sí.* But not good, I think."

Carly pulled a notepad and pen from a drawer. "I'm ready."

He hesitated. "Where Miss Amanda?"

"She's in the hospital with food poisoning." She shared what she knew. "I'll let her know you were asking about her."

"*Gracias.*" He relaxed in his chair. "The police in Iquitos tell me they find the temple. Nobody knew was there before. My friend was first to find it. He said he read history of the area and searched for landmarks. Police found many beautiful paintings. Many passages. Many boxes full of jewelry, gold cups, plates. Statues."

"I can see why your friend didn't want anybody to know about it."

"*Sí.* Is law same in your country? All would belong to government?"

114

She chuckled. "We'd say it belonged to the people."

"*Si*. But people still try to keep for themselves?"

"Yes. I'm sure that happens a lot here, too."

"The *policia* tell me there are five paintings with beautiful necklaces. They search the cave. No necklaces. I think this is what my friend send to Miss Amanda."

"Why would he do that if there were only five? If she wanted more, he couldn't provide them."

"I think he hope she would buy other pieces. Miss Amanda like to sell original pieces, too."

Made sense. "The bill of lading said there were four pieces from your friend. Where do you think the other piece is?"

"Maybe he keep for himself. To sell. Maybe he knows somebody in Peru who wants to buy. Or maybe he planned to take to government and say he found only one."

She jotted down a few notes. "Any idea where he might have hidden the other necklace?"

"No. But I travel to his town tomorrow for his funeral. I will ask if anybody know."

"Be careful, Rogelio. Maybe he died because he found the temple and took the pieces. If whoever killed him learns you're asking questions, you could be in danger."

He grinned at her. "No worries. I just dumb Cusconian. What do I know?"

"Is that like being a redneck in America?"

His brow pulled down. "Redneck. I no understand."

How to explain? "A redneck is somebody who works in the sun and gets a sunburn around the collar or the neck of his shirt."

"Sound like most people in Peru."

"Can you send me any pictures?"

"*Si. La policia* sent me photographs of the paintings. I will send right now." He tapped buttons on his cell phone then grinned at her. "Done."

Her own cell beeped at her, and she opened the app to view the

115

images. Each painting sported a stern-looking man dressed in a luxurious tunic and cape, wearing a simple crown. Around each man's neck, a medallion the size of her palm hung about mid-chest. Decorated with symbols foreign to her, as well as shimmering stones of various colors, each piece unique. A chain of yellow metal—gold?—with links as big as her wedding ring, shone from the antique artwork.

"Wow." She studied each photo again. "These are beautiful." She tapped the first one. "Amanda has nothing like these in her store. I'd have noticed them."

"Thief took before she receive package. Which mean only one thing."

"Actually, I think it means two things."

"Two?"

"He—or she—is seeking the fifth piece. And he—or she—isn't afraid to kill to get what they're looking for."

+ + +

By mid-afternoon, Carly was done with sitting. Not because it wasn't one of her favorite pastimes—add a sweet tea and a good cozy, and she was set—but because her nose for mystery itched to learn more about the Peruvian Connection, as she'd taken to calling it.

Not that this little conundrum was any comparison to its namesake, that brilliant movie of the 1970s. However, the phrase rolled off the tongue easily, and, as she learned today, always brought a smile to Mike's face.

She pushed away from the desk and stood. "I'm going out for a bit."

He grunted. "The last time you went out by yourself, you ate a meal and then disappeared for hours."

"Not hours. *An* hour. If that."

He peered at her. "So, why are you really going out?"

She shrugged. "Don't know." A tap alongside her nose. "It's itching."

He sprang from his chair and rounded the desks. "Means you're gonna have a fight."

She pecked him on the cheek. "Or kiss a fool. There. Feels better already." A smile just for him. "Seriously, I want to talk to the chief. See what's going on with this mini-crime spree. If he has suspects. When the hanging is."

"Uh-huh."

"You don't sound convinced."

"I think you've got something up your sleeve." He lifted the edge of her short-sleeved shirt. "But, it's not very big 'cuz I can't see it."

In appreciation of his bizarre sense of humor, she kissed him again—this time on the mouth. "See you in an hour."

"No eating while you're out."

"Why not?"

"You'll spoil your dinner."

The prospect of not being on kitchen duty brightened her day. "Are you cooking?"

"I am."

"Great." She headed for the door with him close behind, grabbing her keys as she went. Before exiting, she paused and faced him. "I'll bring dessert."

"We have plenty here already."

She waggled an index finger at him. "Never too much dessert on hand."

He waved her off then retreated to the office as she let herself out. If she knew her husband, he'd get so absorbed in something at his desk he'd forget all about making dinner.

In that case, even though they had two pecan tarts and the cinnamon buns, she'd best get a pie or a cake—make sure they had enough if that's all that made it to the table.

She slowed at the end of the driveway. Where did she really want to go? Amanda was still in hospital, so no point going there. Although she could go past Amanda's house. Pick up her mail and newspaper, if she hadn't already made arrangements with a neighbor. Then a jaunt to *Sweet Tooth Bakery,* and that would be enough. She could stop at the police department—a call to Chief Donovan would suffice.

117

Crossing the intersection at Old Tom's Hill and hers, Jamaica, she continued toward the harbor. Tulips and narcissus showed their colors at several houses, reminding her that Spring was around the corner.

After skirting the park, she arrived at Amanda's house, where she picked up two newspapers at the end of the driveway then went toward the front door. Three or four pieces of mail and the weekend flyers filled the small mailbox, so she extracted those, added them to the newspapers, and set them between the storm and front doors.

Good. Her neighborly duty done, she headed back to the main street. Maybe a quick stop at *Dew Drop Inn* for a pick-me-up cup of Victoria's coffee would be a good diversion.

Whether the anticipation of a cup of java or the thought of sitting for a few minutes was responsible for her quickened pace, she wasn't sure. Maybe both.

Then her feet got behind and her torso got ahead, and down she went. Face first, hands out to break her fall. Thud! on the concrete sidewalk.

Her vision swirled, and she laid there, the breath knocked out of her. The heels of her hands stung from their impact with the rough surface. Drawing a couple of deep breaths, she rolled over onto her back. After wriggling her toes and flexing her knees, she pushed herself upright. What a klutz. Now the knees of her pants bore distinctive road rash marks, and her hands were raw and tender.

She glanced around. Thank goodness nobody was in their garden or on the street. Focusing on getting herself to her feet as quickly and genteelly as possible, she rolled again. Once on her hands and knees, she bit back a gasp at the tenderness in both. Standing, she bent at the waist. Another deep breath while the dizziness passed, and she straightened.

Brushing the dust and dirt from her legs, she groaned. How would she explain this to Mike? He wouldn't let her go anywhere without him if he knew. Maybe she could sneak into the bedroom and change outfits while he slaved over dinner. Which meant she couldn't go home yet. She hadn't been gone long enough, and he would certainly question her if she cut her time away short.

Even though they both knew she wasn't out for exercise.

No, he thought—as she had—that she couldn't possibly get into much trouble in an hour in her hometown.

How wrong they both were.

She shook off the trembling in her knees and continued on her way. Surely she'd tripped on a crack in the sidewalk. She knew this part of town like the back of her hand. No reason for her to fall.

She kept her eyes straight ahead, watching where she set her feet, and continued down the street. At the bookstore, she scanned the titles displayed in the windows, deciding before she ever went in. For her, a bookstore was like a liquor store to an alcoholic—one was too many, and a hundred would never be enough.

Three minutes later she exited with two historicals—one about a plane that crashed in Greenland during the second world war, and one about an attempted presidential assassination. She tucked the bag under her arm and surveyed Main Street. Still quiet. Few cars. Nobody window-shopping. She shrugged into her light jacket when the salt-laden breeze crept down the back of her neck.

The bell heralded her departure, and Carly turned right, heading for the diner two doors down. As she passed the *Snip'n Clip*, she caught sight of a portly patron sitting in a chair on the barber shop side of the business.

She froze. The man bore an incredible likeness to Mayor Wells.

But that wasn't possible. He was. . .

The man turned his head and spoke to the man cutting his hair, and she saw instantly she was mistaken. The nose was all wrong, and the hair was too thick. Even his mouth wasn't right.

She blinked a couple of times, hoping to clear away the cobwebs and the memories, then continued on. Maybe she was reading too many mysteries.

A car slowed then pulled to a stop before her, and the passenger window rolled down. She bent to peek in.

Chief Donovan, dark circles smudging beneath his eyes, nodded to her. "Out for another promenade? That's two in the same day."

"You sound like Mike."

"He caught on to you yet?"

"Nope, but we need to stop meeting like this. Folks will talk."

He patted the passenger seat. "Hop in, and I'll drive you home."

"Thanks, but I have to pick up an order at the bakery."

"We can stop there, too."

She opened the door and slid in. Police vehicles fascinated her, and she never grew tired of all the lights and technology. Even a town as small as Bear Cove sported the latest gadgets, and the town council had announced its intention to provide dash-mounted computers soon.

Chief Donovan glanced in his side-view mirror then made a u-turn. "Don't suppose you heard the latest?"

Aha, finally getting down to the actual reason for his wanting her alone in the car. "About?"

"Another break-in at Amanda's shop, and prints found at the park."

"What did they take this time?" She glanced out her window as they passed the pharmacy. "And prints in the park isn't new. Seems like there should be lots of them. It is a public park."

"A necklace. And these prints are like the ones we saw in the alley behind Amanda's shop." He slowed the car and pulled into a spot in front of the bakery then rolled down his window. "Seems the thief targeted one item this time. In the front display case."

Her heart quickened. "The Peruvian display?"

"The same." He shut off the engine. "I talked to Amanda, and she described what should be in the case. The missing piece is a medallion on a gold chain."

This was all wrong. Surely the thief knew this wasn't one of the five from the temple. Why steal this particular piece? She'd have to ask Rogelio about it. Maybe it was a replica? If so, who else knew about the temple and the jewelry? Or were the pieces common to the craftsman of Peru?

She gripped the door handle. "And the prints? Made by the same person?"

120

He shrugged. "Who knows? Hopefully so. Or else it means there are two loonies in our town." He chuckled. "Or should I say, two *more* loonies than is common in our resident population."

"Is the highway patrol doing any analysis on the prints? I know they can do wonderful things nowadays with computer-aided programs. They can tell if a person made the prints, of if they were assembled, so to speak."

He nodded. "Unless there really is a creature in town that has a human foot and a goat's foot. Otherwise, they used some kind of contraption and managed to not leave any prints of their own. Or they hopped on one foot and stamped down the cloven hoof. I've voting for the latter. The booted part of the impression seems deeper than from a simple walking mechanism. But nothing official yet."

"So, whoever is doing this wants us to remember they are still around." She shifted in her seat to face him. "And no stolen vehicles reported?"

"No." He quirked his chin toward the bakery. "Get your stuff. I'll wait then take you home."

When she pushed through the door into the bakery, the bell over the door tinkled, announcing her arrival.

Clara bustled out from the back room, wiping her hands in a cloth. "Hi Carly. What can I get you today?"

Carly scanned the display case. "Can't decide between pecan pie and Black Forest cake."

"Can't go wrong with one of each."

"Better not. Mike will eat too much."

"I have mini versions of each. Like fancy cupcakes."

Carly smiled. "Great. I'll take two of each."

Clara bagged her choices along with two chocolate eclairs for the chief, and Carly paid for it. After returning to the car, balancing the boxes in her lap, she handed him the smaller container. "For you."

He sniffed the box. "Thanks. My favorite. Chocolate eclairs."

"You can tell that by the smell?"

He grinned. "I'm a cop. Doughnut identification is a course every

121

year in the academy."

Sounded like her kind of school. "Really?"

"Just kidding. But they are my faves."

Clara bagged her choices along with two chocolate eclairs for the chief, and Carly paid for it. After returning to the car, balancing the boxes in her lap, she handed him the smaller container. "For you."

He sniffed the box. "Thanks. My favorite. Chocolate eclairs."

"You can tell that by the smell?"

He grinned. "I'm a cop. Doughnut identification is a course every year in the academy."

Sounded like her kind of school. "Really?"

"Just kidding. But they are my faves."

At the corner of Main and Old Tom's Hill, she waved to Jacob as the older man pumped gas into an old farm truck loaded with chicken crates. He returned her greeting, then turned back to his conversation with the driver, an older man in a straw farmer's hat.

He pointed the car toward Old Tom's Hill, turned onto Jamaica, and pulled into her driveway. "Let me know if you come up with anything new."

"Will do."

She stepped out, looped the bag of books over her arm, stacked the dessert boxes, then nudged the door shut with her knee. He waited until she reached the door before backing down to the street.

She jabbed the doorbell with her elbow and Mike opened the door. "I couldn't decide, so I brought two choices."

He eased the boxes from her grip. "I didn't expect you home yet." A glance over her shoulder and he peered at her. "Returned home by the cops? What trouble did you get into this time?"

She mock-punched his overladen arm. "No trouble. I wasn't gone long enough."

He glanced at her reddened hands and the knees of her jeans. "Seems like there's more to your story than you're telling." He stepped aside. "Dinner is in the oven, and I brewed a pot of decaf. Let's relax for a bit and you can tell me all about it."

"There's not much to tell."

As soon as the words were out of her mouth, she rued them.

And judging by the expression on her husband's face, her failure to deny that she had nothing to tell hadn't escaped him.

She sighed. Appeared like her opportunities to go anywhere by herself were curtailed as of now—again.

+ + +

No wonder the woman's hips were so wide. Two desserts. Americans are so hedonistic. Not that there aren't overweight women in Peru, but most weren't so because of indulging in such luxuries.

No. Most carried extra weight from too-close-together pregnancies, or consuming too much high-starch, low nutritional value foods. A curse on the Peruvian culture. On much of South America, where food was scarce and people were poor. Mostly because governments care more about their own status than about their population.

The theft of the jewelry, designed to divert police attention, only heightened the nosey accountant's interest in the case. That much was obvious from their discussion at the bakery. She was well-informed, that one, asking about the footprints. A stroke of genius, that.

Time to move on to the next phase of the mission. Another break-in. Perhaps a death. Continue the cycle of terrorism to keep law enforcement occupied and not focused on the actual purpose: repatriation of what belongs to Peru.

And anybody who tried to stand in the way?

As dust. Here today and gone tomorrow.

Chapter 13

When the alarm buzzed her awake on Sunday morning, Carly stared at the device for a moment. Why had she set the—right. Church. Although neither she nor Mike told anybody else they were planning to attend, they'd agreed the night before it was proper that they followed through on this.

Following a leisurely Full English Breakfast—minus the kippers—she followed Mike to the car. Once inside, she fastened her seatbelt and swallowed back the lump in her throat. "Do you think they'll let us in?"

He chuckled. "Pretty sure they will."

"Why? I mean, we stopped going before."

"I'm pretty sure they offer at least one second chance."

"Ever go to church before I met you?"

He shook his head. "Not unless you count special events. Like weddings, funerals. Oh, and Sophie had the kids christened. She said it was—"

"I know. The right thing to do." She settled back in her seat as he backed onto the street "Still, it feels strange."

Another nod. "Kind of like when we used to take the kids in for their vaccinations. We knew they wouldn't like it, but it was for their own good."

She chuckled. "You know how much I hate needles. I hope this isn't anything like that, or I probably won't be back."

He patted her hand. "Think of it as preparing for a trip out of the country."

"Like to Peru?"

"Right. If you went there, you'd have to have shots for those horrible diseases you don't want to get."

"So, what horrible thing will church protect us from?"

His mouth turned down. "Don't know. I suspect church attendance isn't a panacea against awful things happening."

She sighed. "I wish it was. Then I'd know when I go to the doctor on Tuesday that things will be all right. That my overblown imagination—" She squeezed his hand. "—would be just that. And I'd get a clean bill of health."

"Got a feeling it doesn't work that way."

"I caught one of these religious guys on television last week as I was channel surfing, and he said God isn't a vending machine. Put your money in and get a treat." Another sigh. "Too bad."

He crossed Main Street and pulled into the parking lot of the church. "Here we are." Several spots marked VISITOR were vacant, so he eased into the one furthest from the main entrance. "We could do with the fresh air."

She chuckled. "And yesterday, when I went out twice, you wondered what I was up to."

"Only because I wasn't with you." He nodded toward the building. "There's Victoria."

She pointed. "And Mrs. Olsen. At least we know somebody."

Mike came around and opened her car door, offering his hand to assist her. "Let's enjoy ourselves, okay?"

She exhaled. "I'll try. But you know how I am about trying anything new."

"Yeah. Right up there on your avoidance list, below spontaneity."

"Hey, I can be as spontaneous as anybody, if I'm given enough notice. Like being here today. Planned it for days. And here we are."

Mike held his arm to her. "Shall we?"

She slipped hers through, and they headed for the church. Ahead of them, Victoria waited for Mrs. Olsen, who then turned and beckoned

126

Carly and Mike to join them. All around them, people she recognized from businesses and town meetings streamed past them. The parking lot, which held about fifty cars, was now full.

She pasted on a smile she was sure would flee at the first sign of trouble. "Mrs. Olsen. Victoria. Good morning."

The owner of the diner beamed at them both. "Good to see you. Let's get our seats. Don't want to be late."

Mike gestured for them to go ahead, then followed in their wake.

All the way to the front row.

Carly groaned. Not what she'd planned, for sure. Front and center. No doubt, those who recognized her already whispered behind their hands about a woman like *her* darkening the door of their church.

And those who didn't know her were likely wondering who were these bold strangers.

Still, when Victoria settled on her left, Mike on her right, and Mrs. Olsen beside him, she relaxed a mite. As though the two women vouched for her in some manner. Or like bookends, holding her in place. Upright.

An hour later, the service ended, and she retraced her steps to the door where Pastor Wilkes shook hands and chatted with each before they left.

Another gauntlet to overcome.

But when she reached the man, he gripped her hand in an adequate but not too tight embrace and smiled at her with grey twinkling eyes. "Thanks for coming today."

"Um, thank you. I enjoyed your lecture. I mean, sermon."

Still holding her hand, he tipped his head to one side. "Oh, which part?"

"Well, all of it, but especially the part about not being afraid. What verse did that come from?"

"You'll find a similar theme all throughout the Bible, but today I read from Psalm 121."

"I'll have to research that." Her cheeks heated. "This is only my third time in church. Except for the usual, you know."

"I do." He grinned, and the expression reached every wrinkle and

127

crinkle in his face. "We match'em, hatch'em, and dispatch'em."

"Huh?"

"Weddings, christenings, and funerals."

She liked a man with a sense of humor. Especially one who could make fun of himself and his own vocation. "Nice. Well, I guess we'll see you next week." She glanced up at Mike, who nodded. "Yes, we'll be here."

"If you're free tomorrow evening, you might like to come check out our New Members' Class. Learn more about the church, what we believe. Half-past six, right here." He leaned closer. "We have decaf coffee and doughnuts from the *Sweet Tooth Bakery*."

Mike sidled closer. "You sold me, Reverend."

After the two shook hands, Carly scurried toward their car.

Mike called out. "Hey, where are you hurrying off to?"

"Don't want to get invited to the potluck. Or to join a committee."

He caught up with her and clasped her hand. "You love joining things."

She pulled away from him and shoved her hands into her pockets. "Do not. Now I know you're teasing me. I'm not a joiner."

"Maybe not. But you're a doer. You love helping."

"And that's the kind of people that churches are seeking. Folks who work day and night for free. They want money, and they come right out and ask for it without even a blink of the eye."

"You don't have any problem asking your clients for money, do you? When you do a job they asked you to do. So, why should a church be any different? And were you listening when he spoke about the missionaries they support around the world?" He unlocked the passenger door and held it open for her while she sat. "I think I will like coming here. And I'm glad he invited us to find out more about the church."

After he sat behind the wheel and fastened his seatbelt, he turned to her. "Straight home?"

She shook her head. "Let's sit a minute."

He reclined his seat a few inches. "Something on your mind?"

She stared out the windshield. "What is wrong with me?"

He chuckled. "Don't think I want to sit here that long. Are you going to take notes?"

She slapped at his hand. "Seriously. I'm the one who mentioned the potluck. And I really did enjoy the message. And the music."

He closed his eyes. "Me, too. We could still go in and eat."

"Why didn't I want to stay?"

"I think the introvert in you took control."

"Possibly." But surely there was more to it than that? She turned to face him. "I think He got too close."

Now Mike opened both eyes. "Who? The pastor? Somebody at church?"

"God. I wasn't ready for that. I thought I could take this one step at a time. On my own terms." She clasped his hand. "But I don't think that's the way He works."

Mike returned his seat to the upright position. "Love can be like that."

"What do you mean?"

"Remember when we met? Did we have any intention of falling in love and getting married?"

She shook her head. "We met over drinks at that conference."

"Were you expecting for a lifelong commitment?"

Her brow pulled down. "No way. I was enjoying being single. After coming out of a bad marriage."

"Right. Me, I was busy enough finishing raising the kids, working—I didn't have time for a wife. Or a girlfriend."

"So, what changed?"

"I called you a month later. Remember?"

She smiled. "Right. And I was glad to hear from you. I remember how my heart skipped a beat when I knew it was you." She rubbed the back of his hand. "I'd thought a lot about you for that month. Wondering if I'd ever hear from you again. Hoping I would. Hoping I wouldn't."

"I felt the same way. Hoping you'd answer the phone. Hoping you wouldn't."

She sat back. "When we met up in New York City, I was scared to death. Thinking maybe I'd made up the connection I felt. That maybe it wasn't real."

"But it was. By the end of that weekend, I knew we were together for life. If you'd have me."

"Love." She sighed. "Can't fight it, can you?"

"The pastor said today that God is love. And He loves us completely. Always. No wonder he's chasing us down."

She exhaled. "So, I should simply sit back and let Him catch me?"

He shook his head. "I think it would be better if we turned around and ran back toward Him."

"Do you think we should go back in?"

He turned the key and started the engine. "Nope. I think He's well able to track us down outside the walls of the church." He headed for the street. "Any stops you want to make?"

"Not for me. But I didn't take anything out for dinner."

"No worries. Lots of leftovers from yesterday. I'll warm it while you put your feet up."

She leaned her head back. She *was* tired, but for no good reason. So far she'd eaten and sat. Maybe the stress of a new group of people affected her so much. A dedicated introvert, she enjoyed socializing but needed time to recoup after.

And leftover Italian food was a great rejuvenator.

Would this pattern be her new normal? Resting more, working less? Would she be relieved when she received her diagnosis on Tuesday? And would her physical limitations—whether from illness or age— prevent her from doing what she did best?

If she couldn't solve mysteries, what would she do with herself?

+ + +

After lunch and a nap, Carly nudged Mike, who lolled next to her on the sofa. "Let's visit Amanda."

He opened one eye. "Now?"

"Might as well before she gets out of the hospital. Seems the right thing to do."

He grinned. "Wow, one visit to church, and now you want to visit sick folks."

"That's not why." She smacked his hand that roved up and down her arm, accompanied by a waggling of his eyebrows which meant but one thing. "And save your amorous advances for later."

He exhaled and sat up, then ran his fingers through his hair. "Okay. Let's go. Then we can come back and rest some more."

Ten minutes later, they strode into Amanda's room, a cheery area that overlooked the courtyard below. Carly perched one cheek on the windowsill, while Mike splayed himself in the recliner. Amanda sat on top of the covers on the bed, looking like she was ready for a jaunt in the park or an afternoon in her garden. Except for the IV in her left arm and a large bandage that contained most of her right hand, that is.

Carly gestured to the gauze wrapping. "Not food poisoning, I take it?"

Amanda's eyes widened. "No. At first they thought it was because I was sick after I ate. But then this welt appeared on the back of my hand. And they took some blood samples. Found a high level of a toxin. Asked me if I'd traveled recently. Which I hadn't." She giggled. "At least, not unless Bangor is their idea of a tropical destination. Which it isn't." She rubbed the bandage. "Anyway, I remembered unpacking several items from that box that came from Rogelio. And feeling something prick my hand."

Mike lifted his head and opened his eyes. "What was it?"

"I don't know. Never saw it. I thought it was a paper cut. Or a sharp edge in the packaging material. I kind of forgot about it. And then getting so sick, and throwing up and—" She paused, cheeks pink. "And all that food poisoning brings on, you know."

Carly's stomach did a little flip-flop. She didn't get sick often—at least, not before this most recent health scare—but her last experience with a fast food chili burger was still fresh in her mind. Even eight years later, the three days she and Mike had spent in the bathroom would never be forgotten. "So, when did they figure out it wasn't something you ate?"

"Like I said, when the welt showed. It was like a little burning pimple at first. Then it swelled up. And my arm turned red." She ran a finger up the length of her arm. "Then they said I had blood poisoning."

"You didn't let us know?"

She shrugged. "I was pretty much out of it by then. Apparently this toxin is strong. Can kill a horse if not treated right away. Which is why I got so sick. They didn't recognize the symptoms because they don't see it around here. The insect doesn't like the cold, so even if one is in a package, it dies before the package gets opened because of the low cargo bay and delivery truck low temps."

Carly slid from her perch and crossed the room. "Have you talked to the police?"

"Not yet. Like I said, I was—"

"Right. How did this one survive?"

Mike sat up straight. "Good question. How did it survive the cold?"

Amanda crossed her legs at the ankles. "Don't know. Don't care. I just need it taken care of."

Carly was lost. "It?"

"The insect. It must still be in the box in my shop." She batted her eyes at Mike. "Could you do that for me?"

"I don't know. Maybe you should call in a professional."

Amanda snorted. "Who? Like Spider Busters?"

Carly knew false bravado when she saw it. "I could bring in the box for you, Amanda, since you're so brave, and you could kill it."

Amanda shrank back against her pillow. "No way. The doctor said a second bite could prove fatal."

Mike exhaled. "We'll find it." He glanced toward Carly. "And kill it."

Nice. Not. "What kind of spider is it?"

"Brazilian Wandering Spider. But it's also common in Peru, apparently."

Carly smiled. "If it wandered, it's probably exhausted. We shouldn't have any trouble catching it."

"Don't be silly, Carly, it didn't—oh, I see. Making a little joke at

132

my expense."

An orderly entered the room and checked the IV bag then retrieved the lunch tray on the counter near the bathroom, then puttered around the in-room lavatory.

Amanda settled herself again. "What else have you learned?"

"The chief told me about the medallion in the display case in the window. Surely the thief knew it wasn't an original."

The store owner sniffed. "The price would have told them that."

"Right." Carly sat on Mike's lap, slapping his hand when he groaned and rolled his eyes. "Be quiet. I am not that heavy." She turned to Amanda. "I'm wondering if the markings on the pieces are traditional."

"And what of it?"

"If they are, perhaps they mean something in Peruvian culture. I did some reading about the pieces, and sometimes the designers encoded a treasure map on items they intended to hand down to future generations."

Amanda's head swiveled to face her. "A map? To what?"

"Maybe another temple?"

The younger woman nodded. "I've heard of that, too." She held up a hand. "One minute." She leaned toward the bathroom. "Are you done?"

The orderly departed the room, tray in hand, head ducked.

Amanda continued where she left off. "How will you find out if the medallion can give us some clues?"

Carly wandered to the window. Several patients and their companions strolled the grounds below, while others sat on benches. "I'm planning to call Rogelio and ask. Maybe I'll do that this afternoon."

Mike stood. "We don't want to tire you. When do you expect to go home?"

"Tomorrow or the day after, most likely."

Carly gripped her husband's hand. "Describe the spider."

"Big and hairy."

Interesting.

Sounded just like *El Chullachaqui*.

133

Were there two Peruvian monsters in town?

Or did one assume the form of the other?

If that were the case, which was the genuine one?

See, this was exactly the sort of thing she needed to keep her mind sharp and her imagination active.

For as long as she could maintain both.

Despite any medical prognosis she received on Tuesday.

+ + +

Here they come, the nosey accountant and her tag-along husband. I step back into this doorway so they don't see me. Hold your breath. Melt into the wall. Pretend they are dangerous.

And don't think that simply because I am invisible doesn't mean they aren't aware of my presence.

Listening in on their conversation while disguised as somebody who should be here was ingenious. An abandoned lab coat and a submissive air. But so much information from that simple act.

So, they know about the spider. Well, that can't be helped now. While the shopkeeper's death would have been preferable, simply getting her out of the way for a few days allows for a deeper search of the store. And stealing the medallion, while not in the original plan, was ingenious. Perhaps they'd now go off in search of the meaning of the symbols on that obvious reproduction. However, while of decent quality, years of copying the marks has severely compromised their meaning. Even with knowing the secret, finding its location using those clues will never happen.

They are playing right into my plan.

+ + +

In the car, Carly fidgeted in her seat, rationalizing the creepy-crawly feeling racing up and down her spine. Finally, she could hold her thoughts in check no longer. "Mike, did you get a strange feeling when we left Amanda's room?"

"You mean like a *Hotel California* kind of feeling?"

"No, not like that. Like somebody was watching us?"

He made the turn onto their street. "Nope." After easing into their driveway and shutting off the engine, he trotted around and opened her door. "Stop expecting mysteries where there aren't any."

Inside the house, she tossed her purse on the sofa and headed for her office. "I'll make a quick call to Rogelio then I'll join you."

"If you're not here in fifteen minutes, I'm coming for you."

"Might be sooner than that if I can't reach him."

However, when she connected on FaceLink, Rogelio answered almost immediately. "Miss Carly. Good to see *jou*."

"Sorry to interrupt your Sunday."

"No, is no problem. You go to church today?"

"We did. How did you know?"

He shrugged. "Is Sunday. All people in US are in church, no?"

She laughed. "No, not all. But that's not what I called about."

"Is serious? How is Miss Amanda?"

"Turns out a large spider bit her."

His brow pulled down. "Oh, is bad?"

"She's doing much better now. I want to ask about the markings on the medallions you sent her."

"Markings? No understand."

Carly ran through the list of symbols on the face and underside of the piece as best as she could recall. "Do you know what they mean?"

"No. Most are sacred to the Incans. We copy them from generation to generation. Sun means Incan king." By joining the tips of his fingers, he created an upside down V. "This means mountain."

"So, the squiggly one means water?"

"Yes. And one like zee means lightning. Or fire. Or volcano." He shook his head. "Sometimes mean more than one thing."

"Any idea what the mountain symbol means?"

Another shake of his head, then he smiled. "I remember that mountain has two peaks. Could mean Waskaran."

Carly googled the name. "Does that begin with a W?"

"In Quechan, yes. In *Espanol,* no. I think is spelled Huascarán."

She deleted the word and started again. "Wow, over twenty-two thousand feet. A monster."

"What monster?"

She chuckled again. "No, simply a term for a large anything." She thought about other symbols. "So, the sun could mean a king's temple, on the mountain. And not just any hill, but that one in particular."

"Or could be at base of mountain, like it protects secret. Or might mean where the sun shine through the peaks at certain time of day or day of year."

"Like at Machu Picchu, where the sunbeam shines in through the window onto the altar?"

"*Sí.*" He clicked several keys. "I no find information. But I have friend who works for national museum in my country. I will call him tomorrow and ask him these questions. *Sí?*"

"That would be great."

"Good. I leave in hour to go to my friend's house in Iquitos. I fly to Lima, then fly to Iquitos, then take bus to village and boat to next village. But you call on my cell tomorrow and I tell you what I know."

"Sounds like a plan."

She disconnected the call and made a few notes while the thoughts were fresh in her mind. Perhaps after a brief rest, she'd sit on the rear patio a while. Maybe prune a few branches. Get a little fresh air.

Perhaps that would clear her head so she could put all these clues in perspective.

Because regardless of what Mike noticed—or in this case, didn't— she was certain somebody lurked outside Amanda's hospital room. And if that was the case, she had two looming unanswered questions.

Who?

And why?

Chapter 14

Despite her conversation with Rogelio and plans going forward for him to check into the missing necklace and to seek more information from his museum friend, Carly found relaxation eluded her. After tossing and turning on the sofa and in her easy chair proved fruitless—and more tiring than if she'd put in a full day's work at her desk—around four she bundled up and headed for the back patio.

The setting sun streaked the sky orange and pink, highlighting the clouds with a pale mauve. That particular shade conveyed peace and a coming storm at the same time. The breeze had died down since they returned from the hospital. The bare branches of the birch and alders barely wriggled. Leaves that needed raking skittered across the grass, and up in the corner where the patio covering met the house, a spider web shimmered.

She covered her legs with the blanket from her easy chair, and settled into an Adirondack chair, her cozy mystery in one hand and studied the book's cover. A castle in the background, a cemetery in the foreground, and a shrouded figure emerging from the mist. *Requiem for the Earl.*

She grinned. Just her kind of book. A mystery, a romance, a bad boy, and lots going on all the way through.

Much like her life. Most of the time.

Who was the bad boy in her story? The monster from Peru? Or was the creature more human than mythical? She chuckled at the image of a half-human, half-goat thing choosing a soda on a flight into the country. Ludicrous, of course.

As the sun continued setting and the shadows lengthened, her novel remained in her lap. Gulls screamed overhead about a bit of found offal, reminding her of the animated movie about the lost fish and the seagull scene. *Mine! Mine! Mine!*

Apparently greed and covetousness weren't limited to people alone.

The motion-sensitive light behind her clicked on, and she listened, expecting Mike to sit beside her. When no sound came from the house, she tipped her head, senses on alert. Doc? The neighbor's dog? A stray leaf? Or perhaps nothing more than the spider traversing his web or dangling from a thread. Sometimes those crazy lights were more trouble than they—

Her breath caught in her throat. Was that a footstep? Over there. She remained frozen in place then swiveled her head toward the side of the house where the gate allowed entry into the yard. Another crunch on gravel. Definitely bigger than the poodle from across the fence.

She set her book on the cement and folded the blanket, laying it on the arm of the chair. Standing, she searched the darkening yard—and the silence of evening—for any indication of the source of the sound.

Releasing her breath slowly, she hesitated to step outside the shelter of the house. She should have brought her cell phone with her. Then she could alert Mike. Instead, he remained inside, oblivious to her dilemma.

Should she investigate? Not much she could do from here. Unless she waited for whoever—or whatever—to make their appearance.

And then it might be too late.

Should she go inside the house? Mike was in there. The phone. Locked doors and windows. Those deterrents would keep the intruder outside until the police arrived.

And then what?

No, the question really came down to did she want to confront this—this whatever it was—head on, or did she prefer to live in ignorant fear?

Getting answers to her questions wouldn't come from running and hiding.

She would stand and fight.

Easing to the edge of the patio gave her a better view of the gate. Still closed. If somebody or something gained ingress through there, the rusting hinges would have alerted her. One benefit to Mike not getting out with his trusty oil can often enough.

She searched the perimeter of the yard, following the fence line down to the garden shed in the corner, along the barrier separating their property from the neighbor's on the back. Unlikely anybody would venture into either yard, since both owned dogs that barked at the tiniest activity.

A shadow appeared above the fence adjoining the house that used to belong to James. She stifled a gasp. The dear old man won the lottery then bought the farm before he could enjoy any of the money. The house still stood vacant. If she were trying to surveil somebody, that's where she'd come in.

And apparently this person or thing recognized the advantages of an empty house and no dogs.

The shadow ducked down. Her heart pounded. Now was the time to make her move. She glanced toward the door. Inside? Or out? She shook her head. She'd come too far, was too involved, to back down now. No way would she live with the regrets of inaction.

Bending at the waist, she scurried to the fence where she'd last seen the form. Breathing in small gasps, she pressed a hand into her side when a sharp pain threatened to interrupt the mission. She paused and pressed an eye to the wooden slats, peering between them. Nothing.

She glanced about for a weapon which she should have grabbed before leaving the protection of the house. Now the only tools available were a bamboo stake on her peonies and a one-by-two support on the rosebush trellis.

The stick of wood it was, then.

She yanked at the splintery board, pausing when a nail screeched.

139

She listened. Still nothing. This time she used two hands to grip the wood and eased it from its years-long position. Hefting it in her hand like a machete, she crept along the length of the fence. When he—or she or it—popped up again like *Pop! Goes the Weasel!*, she'd wallop him—or her or it—a good one.

An almost-silent thwack behind her, and she whirled around.

A form stood before her. Either a short person or a tall creature on two legs. All black. Except for the whites of the eyes. Silent as death, it froze. She locked gazes, still gripping her weapon. Slivers of wood dug deep into her palm. Sweat ran down her spine, tickling and chilling at the same time.

Could she breathe? She'd forgotten how. Unable to move. Unable to think. Unable to duck when a movement in the corner of her eye heralded an attack.

Then she was face-down in the cold dirt. She blinked once. Twice. Where was she? A grave? A shallow hole where nobody would ever find her?

No matter. Rest. Close eyes.

Surrender.

+ + +

Mike plugged his laptop in and settled into the chair near the bed. No way was he letting Carly out of his sight. Not tonight. Or tomorrow.

And no matter how much she protested, probably never again.

He glanced at the still form in the bed. Skin white against the sheets. A knot the size of a radish on her right temple. Darkening circle-shaped mark near her eye. She'd have a shiner tomorrow, for certain.

How long had she lain in the garden? What was she thinking, wandering the flower beds in the dark? After all the trouble she'd had this week with dizziness and weakness, she should know better.

And what was he thinking, letting her do it? Although, truth be known, he didn't realize she'd gone out. He thought she was safely wrapped up in a blanket, reading. Or snoozing. While he worked away on—on nothing important, truth be told. Organizing his computer, deleting old files, moving folders to their shared server.

140

He didn't know she wasn't in the house until he went to put the kettle on. And her chair was empty. As was their bedroom. The car was still in the driveway, and her keys hung on the hook near the door, so he was fairly certain she was still at home.

It was then that he'd checked the back yard. The book and blanket confirmed her presence.

But where was she?

Turning on the rear floodlights showed her location immediately. Heart pounding, he'd run to her and felt her hand. Cold. But a pulse was there.

It took him fifteen minutes or so to bring her around, to cover her with the blanket retrieved from where it lay on the concrete. To agree he wouldn't call an ambulance so long as she could lean on him and get into the house. Which consumed another fifteen minutes.

So here he sat, now, at six o'clock. Full darkness outside.

And here, in his heart, the same.

If he lost Carly. . .

No, he couldn't. Wouldn't.

He'd keep her safe. Somehow. Fix it. No matter what the doctor said.

No matter what she said.

And then the message from church that morning returned, as loud and clear as though the pastor stood here in this room.

My help comes from the Lord.

He exhaled. He couldn't be the one to keep Carly safe. She wouldn't stand for it, anyway.

No, he needed Someone bigger and more powerful.

He closed his eyes and prayed. *God, I don't know where to begin. You don't even know me. And I sure don't deserve anything from You. But if You do only one thing for me, please protect Carly. Keep her safe. Make her well. I guess that's it.*

He opened his eyes and stared at the computer screen. He might not be able to force his wife to watch after herself. To stop wandering in the dark. To stop falling and hitting her head on a rock. Or whatever she hit it on. Although there wasn't a rock near where she fell. Now that he thought about it, she'd rambled on about somebody clobbering her over the head. Which was ludicrous. Why would anybody—

Of course. She was investigating this Peruvian Connection, as she called it. And she'd gotten too close and made somebody angry. Or nervous.

Likely both.

He clicked on several keys. Time for him to help her in the way he could best.

Research.

An hour later, he sat back from the laptop then rubbed at the base of his neck where a crick took up residence. Massaging the knot in the muscles eased the cramp, and he checked his notes.

While there was no official record, rumors abounded in the media and in local folklore in the jungle area about a secret society of working-class men. Formed in the late 1500s, the group took it upon themselves to protect Incan artifacts and temples. Guarding their identity, they replenished the ranks through personal recommendations, much like the Freemasons. A person was invited to join because of their interest in all things Incan and an avid demonstration of national pride.

In the 20th century, with the rediscovery of Machu Picchu and the resulting tourism boom from that historic site, The Trawlers, as they became known, took absolute control of keeping Peruvian artifacts out of the public eye. This group, so named both for their ability to locate secret caches of artifacts and their occupational backgrounds, often used fear and intimidation to achieve their goals. There were reports, both official and not, of members traveling to the ends of the earth to repatriate stolen pieces.

Mike saved several of the webpages in case Carly wanted to check them out later, then shut off the computer and set it aside.

She stirred. "Done for the day?"

He perched on the edge of the bed and held her hand. "Finally awake? Sleeping Beauty, I think I'll call you."

"Where's my kiss, Prince Charming?"

He smiled then lightly touched her lips with his. "How's your

142

head?"

She winced when she touched the knot. "Was better before you mentioned it."

"Carly, you mustn't—"

"I didn't fall. Somebody was out there." She held out her right hand, palm up. "I got splinters from the board. Not that it was much of a weapon." She sighed. "I don't know what he hit me with."

"Are you sure it was a man?"

She shook her head then grimaced again. "Note to self. Don't move head." She quirked her chin toward the laptop. "What were you working on?"

"It can wait until tomorrow."

"I'm wide awake, and apart from this bump, I'm fine."

"I found you lying in the dirt. I thought you were—" He swallowed hard, unable to speak the word. "You know."

She smiled, or at least tried to, the attempt a lopsided version. "I know. And I'm sorry. What did you learn?"

He filled her in, and she absorbed his words in silence, not interrupting even once to ask a question. Which was very un-Carly-like. "I bookmarked several pages so you can scan the articles if you like, and I made notes."

She covered his hand with hers. "Thank you."

He stood. "How about hot tea? That's where I was going when I discovered you missing, so I completely forgot about it in all the excitement."

"Sounds good."

"Back in a flash."

As he turned to leave, her cell phone rang. He checked caller ID. "It's the police chief. I'll tell him you're busy."

"No. I can talk to him."

He sighed and handed her the phone. There was no turning off her mind, apparently. But no way was he leaving until he found out the reason for the call.

A minute later he knew everything she did. At least, about why the

143

chief called.

No record of anybody having bought or sold a car in town in recent days. Although why that was important was a mystery to him.

As was why anybody would want to harm his wife.

Sure, there were days she drove him to distraction.

And yes, she was a full-time job.

But this wasn't just serious.

Whatever was going on was murderous.

+ + +

The car engine purred, and heat poured out of the vents in the dash. Despite the old man's warning that neither ran well. Good thing. February in Bear Cove was much colder than in Peru.

What was that nosey accountant doing wandering the yard? In the cold and dark? A simple attempt to listen at a window—and there she was.

An adjustment to the fan and less air flooded the cabin of the car. Time to move before somebody noticed a strange vehicle on their street. One lesson learned from this mission was that hiding in plain sight in a small town proved much more difficult than in a larger city. People here knew their neighbors, their neighbor's children, and their neighbor's cars. Knew when somebody—or something—was out of place.

Which made terrorizing them a little easier. But also meant they called the police sooner, or, like the Turnquist woman, thought nothing of confronting an intruder. Thankfully, she didn't have a gun, or the outcome could have been completely different.

The goal wasn't to kill her. That would cause other problems.

Mostly for her, of course.

Chapter 15

When her cell phone rang before seven on Monday morning, Carly gritted her teeth. She could easily learn to hate these contraptions. Then again, she was at home, so if not the mobile, folks would still call on her land line.

Still, the notion of a ball and chain reference she recently heard about the cellular device rang true.

She checked caller ID. "Hi, Chief Donovan."

"Not too early for you, is it?"

"No. I had to get up to answer the phone anyway." Taking care not to move her head more than necessary, she turned over in the bed, but Mike's side was empty. She ran a hand over the sheets. Cold. He'd been up for some time. Hopefully, breakfast was on his To-Do list. Or coffee, at the very least. "What's up?"

"Your neighbor called a few minutes ago about a disturbance in your yard last night?"

She groaned. Great. Just what she needed first thing today. "That so?"

"Want to tell me about it?"

"No." She propped herself up in the bed, using Mike's pillow to cushion her still aching head and now also sore shoulder muscles. "Next?"

A long, drawn-out sigh from the chief. "Granted, I didn't take Jacob's shooting spree seriously. Even when we saw the prints. Honestly, I thought the old geezer was seeking attention, that's all."

"But?"

"You're right. There's a big but on the end of that sentence. Too many other things have been going on around town. The break-ins. The missing clothes. The stolen car dumped here. Contrived footprints in the park. And now you."

"Me? What do I have to do with it?"

"As your neighbor reminded me, you are always up to your chin in whatever is going on in this town. And apparently, internationally, too."

She shifted position a mite. "What do you mean?"

"I had a call at around five this morning from a Ricardo Alvarez."

"I don't know him."

"No, but he knows a lot about you." The chief's chair squealed. "Your friend Rogelio has been talking to him. Chewing his ear off, if I understood his English. Extolling your abilities and your bravery."

Carly chuckled at the mispronunciation of her friend's name. "In Spanish, the g sounds like an h. Row-he-lee-oh. About what?"

"The theft of the temple artifacts. Let me see." Papers rustled. "Oh yes, the death of his friend. Missing jewelry. A treasure map. And a monster." Another chair squeal. "Hopefully, you see why I'm calling."

"Who is this Ricardo Alvarez?"

"My counterpart in a place called E-kwee-toes."

"It's pronounced E-key-toes."

"Whatever. Anyway, your friend is there asking a lot of tough questions. Kind of backing Alvarez into a corner. Asking him to re-open the investigation into the death of Rogelio's friend."

"Will he?"

"He said he'd check into the details and then decide. To him, appears to be an accident. The guy was climbing along the top of a crevasse and fell in."

"The same place they later discovered a hidden temple? And a cut rope? Seems like a coincidence."

Another sigh. "You could be right."

"Why are you calling me? Other than the call from Peru woke you up? Getting back at me and waking me from my beauty sleep?"

"Well, that entered my mind. But when your neighbor—"

"If she was so concerned, why didn't she call last night?"

"She was watching television and wasn't sure what she heard. By the time she checked, the lights were on and Mike was in the yard, so she figured all was well."

"Why call you today?"

"Nosey neighbor syndrome?"

"Most likely." Carly glanced out the bedroom window which overlooked Mrs. Ivey's house. A long-time widow with a yapping poodle, they nodded to each other in passing, but hadn't ever really connected. Right now, the blonde barker dug at a spot beneath a flowering crabapple tree like it was aiming for China. Maybe the hole would swallow it up. "Did her complaint break the camel's back, so to speak?"

"Sort of. I figured you couldn't be the center of attention from so many directions at the same time, and there not be something going on. Like they say, where there's smoke, there's fire."

"But you're the police, not the fire department. Why this sudden interest? Business slow?"

"No, that's the thing. Business is anything but. And you seem to be in the middle of all of it."

"It's not like I seek out trouble."

"Maybe not, but it seems to find you, doesn't it?"

She smiled. "Have you been talking to Mike again?"

"Not recently. But seriously, something is going on. It's coming at me from all directions, and we're not prepared, as a police department, to divide our limited resources into so many seemingly unconnected areas."

Ooh, at last, the police asking for help. Surely that was the reason for his call, right? "How can I help?"

"Not sure. Keep me in the loop on what you learn. What you're doing. Who you're talking to. Things like that."

"I notice you said seemingly unconnected areas. But now you believe there is a connection?"

"Only one, so far as I can see."

"And what is that?"

"Not what. Who. You. You are the link to all these crimes."

+ + +

Following a healthy breakfast of coffee and leftover pie, Carly contemplated the next item on her own To-Do list. Mike was in the back yard installing motion-sensitive lighting in every nook and cranny.

At her desk, she called PackageExpress, the only delivery company besides the post office that brought packages into town. After misdialing twice—which she blamed on the knot on her head and not her blurry vision—and explaining what she wanted to three different people, they finally transferred her to Victor's route supervisor, a Mr. Coker.

She introduced herself and got right to the point. "Victor has been the driver on the Bear Cove route for a lot of years, and I've never known him to take a day of vacation. And I'm sure he has a bunch saved up. But I think he would have told me if he was taking time off."

The supervisor, who she envisioned as older, thin, and wearing eyeglasses and a plastic pocket protector because of his nasally voice and irritating habit of chomping ill-fitting dentures together as though trying to keep them in place, hemmed and hawed before answering. "I cannot release personal information about an employee to a voice over the telephone. You could be anybody."

And so could you. Like an alien inhabiting Mr. Coker's body. "I appreciate that. And I'm not asking for personal details. I'm simply asking if Victor is okay."

"Why would you care? It's not like he's your friend."

"True. But he is the friendly, personal face of your company. When I think of PackageExpress, I think of Victor. And we've had some conversations. I know his wife passed away some years ago. No children. He has a sister living in Brooklyn. A niece in the military. And he never missed a day's work for personal reasons."

"Well, I don't know. As I said—"

"Yes, I know. You don't know me. You can't tell me anything personal. Well, let me tell you what I know. Or rather, what I've been told. Victor took time off. That's it. Personal days. Maybe vacation. Maybe mental health days."

"There's nothing wrong with his mental health."

The man's snap reply caught her off guard. And raised her interest. "I didn't say there was. That's what we call them when we need a long weekend. You know."

He sniffed. "No, I don't know. Our company doesn't subscribe to that kind of thinking. Unlike other package delivery services that shall remain nameless—" Another sniff. "—our company carefully screens employees and monitors their mental health on an ongoing basis."

"Right. Nice company line. But I was told—"

"And what is the source of your so-called information?"

Should she say? She wouldn't want to get Nate in trouble if he spoke out of turn. Then again, he didn't say much. "The replacement driver said Victor took some personal days."

Papers rustled. A keyboard tapped. More papers moved. "What replacement driver?"

"The one that delivered my package. And the one to a friend of mine. When Victor was off. Last week."

"That's not possible. You must be mistaken."

She drew several breaths and waited for her heart to slow to something less than a gallop. "I'm not mistaken. I talked to him. At my door. I signed for the delivery."

More keyboard tippity-tapping. "Yes, I see the record for the signature. But that's not possible."

She exhaled. Loudly. Conveying her level of frustration with this conversation, she hoped. "Not only was it possible, but you say you have the record there."

"I do. But that doesn't change the facts. Victor didn't make that delivery."

"No, I already told you—so who did, according to your records?"

"Nobody. That's just it. Victor didn't work on the day the package was delivered."

Finally. "Which is what I've been telling you all along. Nate was the driver."

"No, that's wrong."

"It can't be. I saw him. Nice young man. With a tattoo."

"We have nobody named Nate driving that route." Keyboard tapping again. "And the only Nate or Nathan we have driving for us is fifty-eight years old and works in the western part of the state."

"That makes little sense."

"You're right. It doesn't. You are mistaken."

She gritted her teeth. "So, why was Victor off? Was he sick? Or vacation?"

"Victor was, I'm sorry to say, mugged. And his truck stolen. He was missing for over twenty-four hours, before police located the truck in the airport parking lot in Bangor. Which is where we also found him."

Mugged? "Is he okay?"

"He has a nasty knot on his head where his kidnapper struck him and knocked him out. And he's still recovering from a full day of being tied up without food or water."

Hit in the head? Like she had been? "Which side of his head?"

"That's a strange question to say the least."

"Please?"

A long sigh. "If you must know, his right temple. He's still experiencing dizziness, headaches, and nausea. He's lucky to be alive, according to the doctors."

His right temple. *Her* right temple. And she was facing her attacker, which meant their assailant was most likely left-handed. Well, that narrowed it down to around ten percent of the population. "Who delivered the package to me?"

"Perhaps the person who attacked him."

A shiver ran from the top of her aching head to toes that wanted to run. But run where? To think she'd interacted with a mugger—no worse, a kidnapper—and hadn't even known. No, she'd known something was off about this man calling himself Nate. But she couldn't put her finger on what set off her Spidey-senses.

She thanked Mr. Coker and hung up, but not before asking him to convey her best wishes for a speedy recovery to Nate. Then she sat and thought.

150

For a long time.

When she stirred again, she had a plan. Going through what she knew and what she didn't, separating them into two neat lists, had clarified her mind. Given her a sense of direction. Of purpose.

She glanced into the back yard again. Mike, on a step ladder, installed another light fixture on their garden shed. A floodlight, it appeared. She smiled. If she didn't stop him, their yard would compete with the county airport for electricity usage. The entire eastern seaboard could experience rolling blackouts if all those bulbs lit at once.

No, she had to save him from himself.

And the only way to do that was to say she needed to go out.

+ + +

As they headed down the hill toward Main Street, Mike inhaled the tangy air. The sun strove to peek through the cloud cover, but he didn't care. Nothing could spoil their time.

He glanced at his wife, wondering what she was really up to. Despite her innocenter-than-thou look and protests that she simply wanted some exercise, he wasn't fooled. Sure, she'd taken to walking more, but only because he didn't want her to drive until they knew what was going on in her head. And she agreed that neither of them wanted to feel responsible if she had an accident.

But this. This was too much.

Still, he wouldn't turn down the opportunity to hold her hand and get away from his project for a bit. Maybe he could convince her to stop in at the diner for coffee and breakfast. She didn't fool him when saying she had coffee and a handful of nuts for breakfast. Sure, pecan pie had nuts, but not exactly the same, was it?

Not that he had anything to boast about. Half a cup of java and two handfuls of nuts—the remaining tarts—didn't exactly comprise the breakfast of champions, either.

As they neared the corner, a squeeze of his hand alerted him to a slight change of direction. Rather than head directly for food—his unspoken choice—she headed across the street.

He groaned. He was right. She had an ulterior motive. And a

151

determined destination.

Jacob Roy's garage.

He sighed. Trying to talk her out of her chosen course of action would be like trying to steer the Titanic away from the iceberg. Not a chance. Full steam ahead.

He followed in her wake. Thankfully Jacob was a man of few words, so this shouldn't take long. Then again, maybe they were on a fool's errand. No cars at the pump. No vehicle in the mechanic's bay.

He pulled on her hand. "Doesn't appear he's open yet."

In the middle of the street she pulled a right and headed back on a diagonal toward the sidewalk. "You're right."

"Where are you heading now?"

"To the diner, where else?"

His heart warmed at her words. She read his mind. "Marvelous idea. I was hoping—"

"Sure. Where else would he be this time of day?"

And just when he thought—still, no point wasting the opportunity. "Good. I'm hungry enough for a snack. How about you?"

She cackled. "You're always ready to eat."

He tossed her a salute. "Like they say in the Scouts: Be prepared."

He opened the door of the diner and stepped aside to let her go in first. She did, then surveyed the room before heading for a table in the window. "Hi, Jacob."

The older man lifted his head from his newspaper, which he set aside, and nodded. "Carly. Mike. Nice to see you. What brings you out on this fine morning?"

Carly slid in opposite Jacob and Mike sat beside her. He reached across and shook the man's hand. "Out for a stroll."

"Ayuh." The mechanic eyed them. "Worked up an appetite, did you?"

Mike knew sarcasm when he heard it. After all, he was married to the Queen of that realm. "Yeah. It's a long haul down that hill."

"Ayuh. Almost as long as back up." He focused on Carly, and the corners of his mouth lifted a millimeter or two. "Solve our mystery?"

152

"Not yet. See anything else?"

"Nope." He paused when Victoria came around offering coffee, nodding for her to refill his cup. Then he turned to Carly again. "What'cha having?"

Carly winked at him then turned to the owner. "Whatever he's having." She nudged Mike. "And you'd best order the same."

He shrugged. "Fine with me."

Victoria chuckled and moved off after filling their cups, then called to the cook. "Two more like Jacob's."

"Two more Blue Plate Specials. Coming right up."

Mike sipped his coffee. "How's business, Jacob?"

Now it was the older man's turn to shrug. "'Bout the same. Good thing it's only me living on the proceeds." He leaned forward, elbows on the table, and lowered his voice. "'Course, with this monster thing in town, folks is bound to be scared. Stay more to-home."

Monster? Oh yes, the thing in the alley. "Nothing new from the police?"

Jacob's mouth turned down, and he sat back, settling himself into the chair. "Don't 'spect them to do anything, do you?"

Carly patted Mike's knee. "I'm sure they're doing all they can." She sipped her coffee then added more creamer. "In fact, Chief Donovan called this morning and asked for my help."

Mike stared at her. This was news to him. "You didn't—"

Another pat. "Of course not, dear." She smiled up at him. Oh, oh. What was she up to now? "I didn't tell him I was too busy. I said I'd help."

Jacob peered at her. "With what?"

"Well, with the monster. And did you know about the break-ins at Amanda's shop?"

"Ayuh. And the missing laundry." He leaned on the table again. "What else is going on?"

"Well, they found that stolen car."

He settled back again. "Ayuh. From Bangor. Just some kids joy riding, in my mind."

She shook her head. "I think the man who attacked Victor stole the car to get him to Bear Cove."

The mechanic's brow pulled down. "Who is Victor?"

"The PackageExpress driver."

He waved off her words. "Oh, him. I don't order stuff. Buy it local, or from a supplier who drives it out here or sends it by the good old USPS."

"Apparently he was mugged."

Jacob's eyes widened. "You don't say."

Mike stared at her again. When was she planning to share this information with him? "How do you know that for a fact?"

"I called his workplace and spoke with his supervisor. I was worried about him because he never takes a day off."

Still not a good enough answer. "And what do you think that information means?"

"Mr. Coker said I took delivery of my package on the same day Victor was mugged. And he was found the next day tied up and semi-conscious in the back of his delivery truck at the Bangor airport. If this Nate guy ditched the truck there, he needed a new ride."

Mike sighed. Her explanation only confused things more. "Nate?"

She jabbed him in the ribs with an elbow. "The guy who delivered my package. The one with the tattoo."

Jacob perked up. "You can order a tattoo, now? Boy howdy. In my day, you went to a seedy little shop off an alley and—" A flush crept up his neck. "Well, you know."

Carly chuckled. "I've heard stories, yes. Sorry, poorly worded sentence. The package didn't have a tattoo. The delivery man did."

The older man's mouth went slack. Like he'd suddenly remembered he needed to be somewhere else. He glanced out the window then back at Carly, who stared at him like he has three heads.

She reached across the table and touched the mechanic's hand. "Are you okay? Have you seen a ghost?"

His eyes remained unfocused another moment or so before zooming in on Carly again. "Fine. Fine. Just remembered something."

154

Ah, he was right. See, he could read people as well as Carly could. At that moment, Victoria appeared balancing a tray loaded with three plates of food enough to feed an orphanage. She set the dishes on the table then departed, promising to return with coffee.

Mike picked up his fork, but his wife jabbed him again in the ribs. If she kept that up, he'd have a bruise. "What?"

"Jacob likes to give thanks first."

Mike set his fork down and closed his eyes while the older man asked the Lord's blessing on their meal and their fellowship. He sighed. Was that something they'd start doing once they knew what was expected of them if they became members of the church? Seemed like another complete set of rules—do's and don'ts—headed his way. No worries. They'd have plenty of time to learn if they decided to retire.

Or maybe the decision wouldn't be theirs.

Carly fidgeted in her seat, and he waited to take another mouthful of food. What was she up to?

She hesitated a fraction of a second before asking her next question. "Do you ever fix cars up and sell them, Jacob?"

The mechanic eyed her over his coffee cup. "You in the market for a car?"

"No. Just wondering."

He shook his head. "Not any more. Used to when I was a lot younger, and had more energy than money. Now it seems it's not worth it. Folks want something for nothing, you know?"

She nodded. "I do." She half-turned to Mike, and he recognized the ploy for what it was. An attempt to make it seem like she was talking to him, when really she was addressing Jacob. Old, but it still worked. "I saw an advertisement for a mechanic in Bangor who lets his customers use a courtesy car. When their own vehicle is in their shop for repairs." Now she faced Jacob again. "Do you ever do that?"

His fork stilled mid-air, and he didn't lift his eyes to meet hers. He stayed that way a long moment before setting the utensil down and wiping his mouth with his napkin. "That's a strange question. Have I ever offered you a vehicle when yours was in my shop?"

155

She smiled. "No, but I don't live very far, either, so I've never asked."

"Same with most folks in town, too, I 'spect. Never had anybody ask." He wadded up the paper and dropped it into the middle of his uneaten food. "Got to go. Nice chatting with you."

He set a ten on the table under the lip of his plate and scurried out. The chill morning air off the harbor snuck in around the open door, cooling the temperature of the diner by a few degrees.

But judging by the expression on his wife's face, her curiosity thermometer just shot up by twenty or more degrees.

He swiveled to face her. "What was that all about?"

"Not sure." She scraped the last of her hash browns and eggs onto her fork and into her mouth. "But it sure elicited a powerful reaction, didn't it?"

+ + +

Eating at this diner every day could add pounds and inches to my otherwise trim physique. More exercise is required to keep the offensive middle-age spread at bay.

Still, the food is excellent, and the waitress doesn't ask too many questions. And much could be learned about the attitudes and activities of the people of the town.

Where was that nosey accountant going with her questions about lending out vehicles? Had she figured out the connection between the stolen car and the delivery truck? That might have been a mistake, taking the car from the same place as the dump site for the package vehicle.

So what if she understands the relationship between the two? She still doesn't know enough to figure out the final solution. And as long as she is in the dark, she isn't any threat.

Which meant she'd stay out of the matter, if she knows what is good for her.

And if she doesn't—well, that bridge would be crossed—or blown up—when necessary.

Chapter 16

As soon as she returned home, Carly headed for the phone in her office. Sure, she could have used her cell, but this way she could take notes if needed.

The chief answered on the first ring, and she got right down to business. "Chief, remember our call of early this morning?"

"I do. I was wondering if you did."

She pulled her notes closer. "At one point, I hoped it was a dream."

"More of a nightmare, I'm sure."

"Something like that. But then I realized this partnership of ours was good for both of us."

He cleared his throat softly. "Don't know as I'd call it a partnership. People might tell you things they wouldn't share with law enforcement, so I was hoping if you learned something that could be important to our investigation, you'd tell me."

She peered at the handset. Had an alien overtaken the police chief's body? "Somebody in your office with you?"

"That's right, Carly. Just a minute." Muffled voices in the background, then the door opened and closed. "I'm back."

"Wow, you had me going there for a minute. Thought I had the wrong number."

"A surprise visit from the state trooper's office. Who, as you well know, don't take kindly to sharing information with civilians. Or having said non-law enforcement involved in investigations."

"Right, right. No worries. I won't tell anybody you asked for my help."

"I wouldn't exactly call it asking—"

She wasn't about to let him off the hook so easily. "That's precisely what you were doing, and I am calling to let you know I have information. To help. You."

"Oh, well that's a different story." His chair squeaked—she really should mention that—as he changed positions. "Go ahead."

"PackageExpress has a truck that delivers to town as part of their route."

"I know. We use them for transporting evidence to and from the state crime lab."

"And as long as I've lived in Bear Cove, the same driver has worked the route. Never takes a day off. In fact, he's proud of the fact. No sick days. No vacation."

"Married to his job, is he?"

"Something like that. His wife died many years ago, and they don't have children, so I guess he'd rather wear out than rust out, as my father used to say."

"Cute Carly-ism. Mind if I use it?"

"As much as you like." She leaned back in her chair. "Imagine my surprise when a different driver delivers a package to me and to Amanda a few days ago."

"And this is strange because?"

"I asked Nate about Victor, and he was pretty vague. Said he was taking time off."

"I repeat my question. Why was that enough to rouse your suspicion?"

"First of all, as I said, Victor never takes time off. Secondly, I saw him the previous week, and he never said he was going on vacation."

"Maybe he was sick. Or tired. Or both."

"That's what I thought, too. So, I called his route supervisor."

A long sigh. "I am not going to ask how you know his

158

supervisor."

"Well, I don't. Or I didn't. Took me three transfers and twenty minutes on the phone to track him down. Even then he didn't want to tell me anything."

"Imagine that."

"Do I detect a note of sarcasm?"

"Hopefully, more than a mere note. Continue. I know this is coming to a point. At some point."

She frowned into the phone. "Victor wasn't sick. Somebody mugged him. Hit the poor man over the head. Then tied him up and kidnapped him. And the crook did his rounds here in Bear Cove for him."

"Why would he do that?"

"I think he was searching for something. Or somebody."

"In a package?"

She groaned. "No, not in a package. Well, yes. Something in a parcel, and maybe somebody who received a delivery. Like Amanda, for example."

"Was this something the jewelry items we've been talking about?"

"Yes. I think he removed the pieces he wanted from the box, taped it up, and delivered the rest to her."

"Then what happened?"

"He drove the van to the Bangor airport then stole the vehicle you found later here in town."

"Not very smart. Lots of cameras at those parking lots."

"Right. With the resolution of peering through the bottom of a soda bottle."

This elicited a chuckle. "I get your point. So he's—" Another change of position accompanied by a squeal. "Wait a minute. How do you know it's a man?"

"Well, the driver who came to my door was a man. Nate. With a tatt on his hand."

"Nice street creds."

She grinned into the phone. About time he knew she wasn't simply another pretty face. "Thanks, but we're getting off topic here."

"And you're pretty sure the driver, the kidnapper, and the car thief are the same?"

"Could be three different people." She hated admitting the possibility, since that now tripled the number of criminals on the loose in their town. "But I'm hoping not. Bear Cove would be crawling with crooks if that were the case."

"True. Can you describe the tattoo?"

"Yes. It was like a rough outline of a fishing boat. A trawler, actually."

"And you know that because?"

"Because I live in a fishing town that sends its fleet off every year with a big ceremony." She sighed. Did he think she was an idiot? No, better not go there. "Besides, THE TRAWLERS was written under the image."

"Point taken. I'll check with the state patrol's gang squad. Maybe even connect with the Bangor PD. Anything else?"

"Nope, that's it." She glanced up as Mike entered the office bearing two cups of coffee. She held up a forefinger to indicate she'd be with him in a minute as he set one java before her. She blew him an air kiss then checked her notes. "Got anything to share with me?"

"No updates. We're still plodding along here. Keep in touch though."

The line disconnected, accompanied by dial tone. She hung up the phone.

Some partnership. She doing all the giving, and he the taking.

Still, being knee-deep in another mystery was reward enough.

For now.

+ + +

When the phone rang after lunch, Carly snatched up the receiver. "Amanda. How are you doing?"

"Much better. They said they'll likely let me go home this afternoon. Any chance I could get a ride?"

"Sure. No worries. What time?"

"In about an hour should work. And Carly, I have another favor

160

to ask."

Mike glanced across the desk at her, and she turned her mouth down. He pantomimed something, but she couldn't interpret the gestures, so she focused on the call. "Can't make any promises, but ask."

What would the woman require this time? If the favor involved cleaning, shopping, or yard work, the answer was no. Anything else, maybe. Coming for dinner, absolutely and when?

"I was wondering if you had a few hours each day you could open the shop? I've had several customers call, and I know I'm losing a lot of business." An audible gulp traveled the line between the hospital and her house. "You could take your laptop and work in between customers. I'd be ever so appreciative."

"I'll check my calendar and get back to you."

At which point, said document slid across her desk. Mike. Helpful as always. She glanced at the next few days. Apparently she was free as a bird. Apart from her doctor's appointment on Tuesday, of course. Which wild horses wouldn't drag from her mouth.

At least not to the Chatty Cathy of Bear Cove.

She penciled in the events. "I could go in from ten until noon, if that works."

"Great. I sure appreciate it. See you in an hour."

She hung up. "Thanks. You roped me into spending two hours each morning at Amanda's shop. At least for a few days. Until she's recovered." She tossed the pencil on the desk. "Then again, it will give me the chance to poke around. Search for clues. Solve the mystery." She beamed at him. "Be the hero again."

He shook his head. "The humble hero. Don't forget that."

"Right." She turned back to her computer. "Better clear my desk. We have the meeting tonight, then we see Doc Walsh. You can drop me off at the shop. I'll ramble on home when I'm done. Maybe pick up dessert along the way. Have a hearty meal before my appointment in the afternoon."

"We don't need—" He chuckled. "You're the only person I know who can gain weight while exercising."

161

An hour later, she filed the last few receipts for home expenses when her computer beeped to let her know she had an incoming video call.

Her favorite Peruvian appeared on the screen. "Miss Carly, how are *jou?*"

"Doing great, Rogelio. And you?"

"Good. *Si. Muy bueno.*"

"Do you have information for me?"

"*Si.* I am here in Iquitos. I ask around and know where my friend live. I go there tomorrow."

"Good. Anything else?"

"*Si.* I ask around about The Trawlers. Nobody want to talk about them. Are afraid. Say bad things happen to people who ask too many questions."

"Understood." Well, that was disappointing. "Thank you for trying."

"I do learn they are not in Peru. But they come from my country. They are—how do you say?" He turned and fired off a question to someone off-camera. Several back and forths later, he turned to face her again. "*Mi esposa,* Carmen. She come with me. Her English better than mine. She say the word I seek is enforcers. You understand?"

"Yes. They are dangerous."

A rapid bobbing on the head. "*Si.* Very dangerous. They beat people and frighten them."

"Are they in the US?"

"Oh, *si.* And they wear markings on their hand to show their loyalty."

"A tattoo?"

"*Jes.* Tattoo." He held up his hand and indicated the space between the thumb and forefinger on the back of the hand. "Here. Like a boat. On left hand. Closest to heart."

Nate's hand flashed in front of her eyes. Left hand. "Why a boat?"

"They sometimes smuggle artifacts into our country. Drop off coast and pick up with certain kind of boat. *Barco de jabeguero.*" He turned to Carmen again as she translated for him. "Trawler. Boat with long arm that pulls net behind. Is how they retrieve packages thrown overboard."

The Trawlers. Explained the name and the tattoo. "Got it. Thanks, Rogelio. Stay safe. Both of you."

While not exactly new information, Rogelio's call confirmed what she already suspected.

She was up against the Peruvian equivalent of the CIA.

Only more corrupt. Less disciplined.

+ + +

At seven-forty-five that evening, Mike pulled into the driveway and parked. He turned to face Carly. "That was interesting."

"I wouldn't describe my tripping in a crack in the sidewalk as we entered the church interesting. It was humiliating." She groaned. "What must they think of me?"

He laid a hand on her forearm. "First, the lighting was really bad. And secondly, only a couple of people saw you stumble."

"They probably thought I'd been tippling before the meeting."

He smiled. "I'm sure they didn't. And no doubt they'd forgotten about it by the time we left."

"Is that the explanation for the huddle of potential new members at the top of the stairs? Nobody dared go down ahead of me in case I fell." She chuckled. "What a vision. Like holy bowling."

"That's my Carly." He nodded toward the house. "Ready to go in?"

"Let's sit for a few minutes. Until the car gets too cool." She stared out the passenger window. "What did you think?"

"About the meeting?" He settled back into his seat. "Or about your recovery?"

"The meeting." She slapped at his hand. "Although I managed to stay on my feet."

"Yes, you did." He exhaled. "So, the meeting. I liked what I heard. I appreciate the conservative stance the church takes on spending, hiring, and expansion. But I also like that they're open to folks starting new ministries and groups. Sounds like a good fit for us."

163

"Yes, it does. I like the pastor. He is personable, can manage a meeting well, stick to the agenda while giving folks the chance to take part."

"But?"

She turned to face him. "Why do you say that?"

He shrugged. "I don't know. I sense a but coming."

She grinned. "Actually, no. I'm ready to join the church. If you are."

Her response surprised him. She wasn't a joiner. One on one she was fine. But Carly rarely sought out larger groups. But to be honest — "I went there tonight to figure out if I wanted to join a church at all. This one in particular. But that's not what I really want."

She tipped her head a few degrees to one side. "You don't want to become a member?"

"Right. I want more."

Her brow pulled down. "A member of more than one church?" She snorted. "Wow. That's a gigantic step. I don't know if you can really—"

"No, silly. More than simply being a member. More than simply showing up on Sunday morning. I want something more."

She nodded. "I know what you mean. It feels like we're deciding to get married. Like this is a life commitment. And exactly like marriage isn't about a piece of paper or even us saying we're a couple, this is different."

She got it. She got him. Another reason he loved this woman so much. He breathed deep to make room for how much his heart swelled at that moment. "Exactly. Pastor Wilkes talked about being part of the family of God as well as the family of First Church of Bear Cove. That's what I want."

"Me, too. I hope they'll have me."

"And me." He gripped the steering wheel. "But how do we do that?"

She pulled out the pocket testament given to them by a Gideon at church that evening. "Larry told me the most important pages in this

164

book were the last two. Let's see what they say."

Together they perused the verses listed, the ones that talked about their need for a savior and how God provided the solution to their sin problem.

Together they prayed the prayer.

Together they remained in the car, holding hands, long after the vehicle chilled.

Chapter 17

Tuesday morning, Carly got the jump on the chief and called him at one minute past seven. This time the phone rang seven times—she counted them—before he answered.

"Oh, did I wake you?" She could afford to be all sugar and pie to him, since she initiated the call. From her kitchen. "Or have you been up for hours?"

"Minutes, at least. And I am at the station. Just returned from fetching another cup of the vile black stuff they call coffee around here."

"Hands full of doughnuts, too?"

He grunted. "Contrary to popular belief—"

"I know. Not all cops eat them. I figure you more for the bagel-and-cream-cheese type."

"Actually, éclairs, as you remember."

"Right. I'm calling with more information, although I don't know if it will be of any help to you. Maybe it's more in the category of background."

"Go ahead. I'm all ears."

"The Trawlers are a gang that goes to other countries to retrieve artifacts and historical items and documents." She filled him in on the origin of the group as well as the other details regarding replenishing ranks and their terrorist-like mentality. "I wouldn't put it past them to send somebody here to retrieve the samples they believe were stolen and removed illegally from Peru."

"Interesting. Tells us we aren't up against your ordinary run-of-the-mill thug."

"No. I suspect they're very well trained in covert operations, surveillance, illicit entry, search-and-seizure—"

The chief crowed. "You watch way too much television, Carly."

"I hardly watch any."

"Then you need to broaden your horizons. If I didn't know better, I'd think you were a cop-wannabe."

"Are you kidding? And get bogged down with all that Miranda warning stuff? Not to mention the way judges frown on entrapment. And what about waiting on search warrants? No way. I have my methods, and they've worked well for me for a long time."

"Right. But this guy is serious stuff. Watch your back."

"Why, Chief, isn't that what the police department is supposed to do? Protect and serve and all that?"

"As I said. Keep a low profile. This person is a professional. Perhaps a killer. Way out of your league."

She chuckled. "Nobody is out of my league, Chief. Because I'm in a league of my own." She leaned back in her chair. "Do you think this person is the one who mugged Victor?"

"Possibly. You might have seen him face to face. Which makes him even more dangerous."

"Nate? He didn't seem deadly. Serious perhaps. Evasive, for certain."

"Well, he knows where you live. Remember that."

She thought back to the intruder in her yard. Was that Nate? She couldn't be certain, but she didn't think so. Then again, she hadn't really paid attention, had she? At the time, he was simply a curious anomaly. With a strange tattoo.

Then again. . .

She smiled across the kitchen table to Mike, who poised the coffee carafe over her cup. "Yes, please."

"Huh?"

"Sorry, Chief, Mike was offering me coffee. You were saying?"

"Nothing. If that's all for now, I have a nasty guy—or three, depending on your theory of what's been happening—to catch. Keep me updated."

"Will do. And hopefully this partnership goes both ways, right? You'll call me if you learn anything else."

"Don't I always?"

Before she could reply in the negative, he disconnected. She stared at the phone a moment before setting it on the table. "I feel like I'm getting the short end of the stick here."

Mike slid into his seat opposite her and dished out scrambled eggs for himself before pushing the bowl toward her. "How so?"

"Seems like I give him information, and all he gives me is grief."

"A policeman's lot is a sorry one."

"Old engineering saying?"

He shrugged. "Nope. Just made it up." He shoved a slice of bacon into his mouth, chomping it into small pieces like a tree going into a mulcher. "Think it will make me rich and famous, once people start using it?"

She giggled. "A hundred-aire, at least." She added the limp slices of bacon he prepared especially for her to her plate. "Seriously. Being married to him would be like living in a convent. No talking. No sharing."

"He'd probably make a much better husband than you're giving him credit for."

She nodded then ate a forkful of eggs. "What's on your schedule for today?"

"Not much. Some paperwork to complete a report. Going to check our finances and retirement savings. Then I want to call the pastor and find out our next step. And we have your appointment later this afternoon."

The next step. Doctor's appointment. Wow. Plenty of decisions to make today. Maybe. Depending on what Doc Walsh said. Too bad that wasn't on the top of her To-Do list. In her experience, medical appointments later in the day tended to not happen on time. Sick people could be so inconsiderate, sometimes. Coming to the office and expecting to be seen right away. Completely oblivious to those waiting their turn. Reading last year's *Better Homes and Gardens*. Or worse yet—she shuddered—a fishing or golfing magazine.

Depending on how her visit went today, maybe she'd buy a subscription to a worthwhile and interesting periodical for Doc Walsh for Christmas. Like *True Forensics*. Or *Cop Talk*. That should liven up the waiting room experience.

"How about you?"

Her husband's words broke into her daydreaming. "What?"

"I said, what's on your calendar for today?"

"I promised Amanda I'd go into the shop for a couple of hours, which I will do after breakfast and a shower. Then I have a few hours until we see Doc Walsh. That's it. Quiet day."

He chortled and refilled her coffee. "We haven't had such an afternoon since we've been married, let alone an entire day." He shook his head. "Nope. I predict you'll find a way to put yourself into danger or find trouble before lunch."

She stuck out a hand. "Want to bet?"

"I'll take that on, since I'm bound to win."

"Okay. Loser buys lunch."

They shook then stood to clear the table.

No way was she a loser.

Lunch was on him this time. And she planned to have dessert, too.

Just you wait and see, Mike Turnquist.

+ + +

At ten o'clock, Carly waved goodbye to Mike as he pulled the car onto Main Street and headed for home. She entered Amanda's shop and switched on the lights. The chill retail area emitted an air of abandonment. And something else.

She sniffed the dank air. An overly ripe banana lingered somewhere. Perhaps in a trash can or on a shelf? She picked up the stack of envelopes and catalogs from the floor beneath the mail slot then continued through to the back room. Amanda maintained the coffee maker and the small work area where she kept supplier invoices and paperwork related to the shop. She sniffed as she went.

Aha. The culprit rested in a basket on top of the mini-fridge, along with an apple and an orange, both covered in green fuzz.

She set the mail on the desk and snagged all three fruit and dropped them in the trash can, which she then set near the back door. Likely she'd find other stuff to discard into the dumpster, so she'd make one trip.

On the shelf over the desk was a box covered in shipping labels and import stamps. Must be the packaging for the order from Peru. She retrieved a pen to poke through the packaging materials, composed mainly of old newspapers, crumpled and wadded.

Whoa, what was that? She snatched back her hand when something dark skittered from one corner to another. What she really needed was a pair of tongs. Or giant tweezers.

Or a hazmat suit.

She drew a deep breath and let it out, then moved other papers until she exposed the corner.

And the creature curled within it.

At least an inch long in the body, black, hairy.

How to kill it?

She scanned the room, wishing for a flamethrower. Or a machete.

But all she had was this pen.

Fine. She'd faced down bigger threats and overcome. Mobsters with guns. Best friends with pillows. A car loaded with explosives.

Another breath for courage. Then she jammed the pen into the recesses of the box, through the spider's body. The legs unfurled—at least two inches long each—and writhed as though trying to extract her weapon.

She snatched her hand back, a shiver running up and down her body amid images of clashing mandibles clamping on her finger. Her hand. Her arm.

Her throat.

After about three minutes, the creature ceased its movements.

171

Now for a way to carry it to the hospital for the doctors to confirm the species so they could be sure they were treating Amanda with the right anti-venom.

A to-go coffee cup, retrieved from the trash beside the fridge, complete with a lid. Even if the little beastie was just playing possum, the sippy-hole was too small for escape. Working slow and easy so she didn't mangle the carcass—which could hinder identification—she slid the body from the pen. It landed with a soft thunk in the cup, and she clapped the lid on immediately.

The pen went into the same receptacle the paper cup had come from. No way would she want to use a pen smeared with spider guts.

She stared at the cup. Seemed weird—like Twilight Zone spooky—to keep it here. Maybe near the front door so she could grab it on her way out? Done.

On her return to the work area, she riffled through the envelopes and other mail. Nothing that couldn't wait. No final notices or Guido-the-knee-breaker letters. She set the pieces aside then decided a cup of coffee was in order. On a trip to the employee washroom to fill the carafe, something caught her attention.

She paused near the back door. A rustling noise? Had that dreaded spider really resurrected? Even now did it stalk her, waiting for her to return to the retail area?

She snickered at her silly thoughts. The creature was dead.

Or was it?

She peeked through the curtain separating the two parts of the store. The spider-carrying cup sat in the same place, lid firmly in place.

Silly indeed.

She returned to her original mission: water.

Another noise, this time more of a metal on metal scrape, froze her in her tracks again. A cat in the trash? Kids trying to break in?

Carly set the coffee carafe on a box and unlocked the deadbolt, yanking the door open. "Whoever is out here—"

A dark form filled the doorway. At least, that's how it seemed to her. At least six feet tall and about as wide. Face covered with a mask.

Dressed all in black.

Was she having another blackout? Was she losing her mind?

If so, this hallucination managed to take on physical form, unlike any other she'd experienced.

It grabbed her by the shoulders and pushed her back into the shop.

It squeezed hard, sending a shaft of pain down through both arms.

And it spoke.

"Don't make a sound."

She wasn't sure she could have forced a squeak past the lump in her throat. Or that she'd have been able to draw enough breath to blow out a match.

Instead, she obeyed his command.

Chapter 18

While following orders was never Carly's strong suit, she figured she'd do as she was told this time around—to a point. After all, the guy was as big as—as Bigfoot. Or so he seemed.

Keeping both hands on her shoulders, he kicked the door shut behind him. The silence created a vacuum-like effect, sucking all the air from the room. Along with her opportunities for escape. What did this guy want? Did he target Amanda's shop because he thought it would be closed? In which case, he had to know she was in the hospital. And if this was a random burglary, he may not know she wasn't Amanda.

Hopefully he didn't ask her a question she couldn't answer. Because if he discovered who she was—or wasn't—that might not bode well for her longevity.

They faced each other for what seemed like hours, but was more like twenty seconds. If that. Then he broke eye contact with her and checked around the work area before returning to peer at her through the knitted mask.

Maybe she could reason with him. "If you want cash, there isn't any."

"Shut up." He shook her then pressed her backward another couple of steps until she came up against the desk. She glanced at his hands on her shoulders. Gloves.

Snap.

"Where is it?"

"Where is what?"

"The necklace?"

"What—"

This time his left hand encircled her throat. "Give me what I want, and you won't get hurt."

She pried his fingers from their grip. "If you kill me, you'll never find it."

He stepped back and released her. "Give it to me."

"What are you looking for?"

"You know."

"If you're talking about the Peruvian items, it never arrived."

"No, because I took them. There were supposed to be five, but I only got four."

She leaned on the desk, unsure her knocking knees would hold her upright any longer. "You took the others?"

"I know you have a reputation for poking in where you don't belong, but I'm not here to play games. You have something that belongs to my government. I never fail on a mission. I will have the item, or I will have your life." A handgun filled his left hand before she could blink. "You will get it."

He knew she wasn't Amanda. Sticking your nose in. Did he know where she lived? Of course he did. It was the man in her back yard. "It's not here."

In fact, she had no idea where *it* was. This man's admission that he took four, not five, necklaces from the package was a wrinkle in her investigation. If he didn't have it, then who did?

He held the muzzle to her forehead. "Then you die now. You are of no use to me."

She raised her hands in surrender. "But I could get it. Have it here this afternoon."

Oh, where did that come from?

He lowered the gun. "Three o'clock. And don't try anything funny or you will die. Understand?"

She nodded. "Three. I'll be here."

"Turn around."

She hesitated. If he was going to shoot her in the back, she wouldn't give him the satisfaction of obeying.

"Turn around or I shoot you now."

Wishing a witty comeback would make its appearance—one that wouldn't tick him off so he shot her dead here and now—she turned so her back faced him. Her heartbeat filled her ears, and she counted each one, grateful for the opportunity. Ten. Eleven. Twelve.

The back door swished shut, and she whirled around and hurried over to open it. A glance left and right. Nothing. The alley was empty.

He was gone.

But his words—and threats—lingered on.

No doubt about it. She needed help.

But who to call first?

Mike? He'd insist she come home and not return for the meet.

The chief? He'd make her step aside and stop investigating the matter.

Amanda? She'd find some way to make this all about her.

No, she needed to ask her new best Friend.

She sat at the desk and bowed her head.

And prayed.

+ + +

Twenty minutes later, Carly stepped out from behind the counter in the retail area, Mike grunted. "Stay back there."

And when she glared at him, he bit back a grin. She could be so infuriating at times. Didn't she understand he was trying to keep her safe? "Back. That display case needs attention."

He'd arrived at the shop within three minutes of disconnecting after she called him. No doubt he'd broken every speed limit on the way, but thankfully neither town cop was on patrol. News that a stranger broke into the store and threatened her didn't really surprise him. In fact, given how much she'd poked her nose into this matter, it was a miracle nobody tried to kill her until now. Maybe she'd been granted an entirely new set of nine lives.

He pulled another box toward him and rifled through it. No necklace. Nothing that seemed anything like what this guy was searching for. He crossed to the Peruvian display. Earrings, bracelets, something that resembled like a hammered copper collar. No necklace.

He turned back to his wife. "What does he want?"

She shrugged. "I told you what he said. Necklace."

"Can you describe it?"

"Rogelio said a large link chain, gold. And a disk about as big as the palm of his hand." She held her hand toward him and made a circle with her other forefinger. "That size. Maybe."

He dusted off his hands. "Nothing here like that." He quirked his head toward the work area. "Let's check in there."

"Can I come out of my cubby?" She straightened a display of bracelets or whatever those solid bands were that women wore around their wrists. "How fun."

When she got within reach, he wrapped his arms around her and pulled her close then rested his chin on the top of her head. "I love you. And I worry about you getting yourself into something you can't handle."

She peered up at him, her chocolate-brown eyes adopting an innocent expression. "And I love you. Didn't I call you first?" She dropped her head. "Well, almost first."

He held her away from him. "Who did you call before me?"

"Not really a call." She met his gaze. "I prayed."

"Oh. Well that's all right then." He snuggled her close again. "I'll admit I was whispering a few words on my way here, too. For your safety. That I wouldn't get pulled over for speeding and running every stop sign."

"Of which there are only two."

"Regardless." His heart welled up again, like the Grinch's in the Christmas cartoon classic. "I couldn't stop thinking of you alone in the store. Strange men breaking in."

She stepped away and shook her head. "Not a stranger. I'm pretty certain it was the guy in the yard the other night. And he's left-handed, too."

A wave of bile and grit and spit rose in Mike's throat. How dare this man come into their town, into this shop—into their lives—and threaten his wife. If he ever got his hands on him, he'd—what? Kill him? Beat him?

No, that wasn't in his nature. He'd protect Carly, of course, if she was attacked. But to out and out chase some guy down and—

He glanced out the window as he struggled to slow his breathing and calm his thoughts. Standing across the street, staring at the shop, a man. He froze and whispered to his wife. "What was the man who came in here wearing?"

She turned. "Dark clothes. Black maybe."

"Don't turn around. Wait until I go out, then lock the door behind me. Make sure the rear door is locked, too. And keep your phone in your hand."

"What's going on? You're scaring me."

"Do as I say."

Heart threatening to trip itself up in its rapid beat, Mike eased out through the door, waiting until the deadbolt clicked behind him.

Good girl.

He paused in the doorway, eyes on the man in black across the street, leaning nonchalantly against a light pole. Trying to appear unconcerned. Blend in with others on the sidewalk.

Except this guy was concerned. The set of his shoulders. The way his eyes never left the shop. The darker skin. Shorter, more compact build. Tense posture.

Mike checked both ways for traffic, then trotted across the road toward the man, waving as though he recognized him. "Hi. Good to see you again."

The man straightened and glanced around. Realizing Mike was heading straight for him, he turned left and strode toward the waterfront. Mike increased his speed to a jog, and the man broke into a full-out run. His own arms and legs pumping, lungs gasping for another breath, Mike followed him.

At one point, the stranger glanced back over his shoulder, almost

179

colliding with a telephone pole. Instead he struck his shoulder, veered left, and careened over a small picket fence. Mike rounded the yard and headed down the lane in the direction of the water. And the town's small marina.

His quarry made a right before the pier. Mike pounded after him, wishing he'd done more cardio workouts, his chest heaving and brain fogging. He sucked each lungful of air in through his mouth. Was this what runners meant about hitting the wall? If so, this particular obstruction was as high and wide as he could see.

Past the marina containing three fishing boats, and another right. Would the man keep them running around in circles? Or rather, blocks?

Just when he didn't think he could drag in another breath, an engine started.

He turned the last corner as a compact car pulled out in front of him, leaving him in a cloud of exhaust and dust. No license plate. He peered through the fumes. No temporary tag. Not even a good look at the car before it took the next turn toward Main Street. Within minutes, the stranger could be on the highway and beyond reach. Which, if he stayed that way, would be fine with him.

He leaned against an outbuilding a moment until his heart rate slowed enough so he could breathe through his nose again. Then he pushed off, straightened, and trudged back toward the store. Every muscle and joint ached with the exertion, and he chuckled at the sorry picture he must make. Then he focused on his—no, their—next step.

By the time he reached the shop, he'd come to four conclusions. One, he didn't want to live in fear of this guy returning. Two, he was pretty certain the thief, the mugger, the man Carly agreed to meet, and this guy were one and the same. She was right. Bear Cove was too small a town to have more than one crook at a time.

Three, Carly had chosen the exact right thing to do before calling him. They both needed to spend more time in prayer to figure out what to do next.

And four, this guy would not get away with terrorizing his wife. Or any of the other nasty stuff he was doing.

For that, they'd need to call in the big guns.

First, God. And then, Chief Donovan.

+ + +

Safe at home and in her office once more, Carly raised her head and opened her eyes when Mike uttered the final amen. A sense of peace overtook the panic bubbling beneath the surface of her mind, and she smiled. Still not sure God was at work in their lives, she was sure of one thing: believing He was made all the difference.

When her computer buzzed and Rogelio's image popped up, she clicked to open the program. "Hi, Rogelio."

"Miss Carly. How are *jou?*"

"Good. And you?"

He held up a disk the size of a pork chop. "I find this in ceiling of my friend's house."

Carly gasped. "It's beautiful. But he only sent four?"

"*Si.* I think he keep one for himself to sell privately. Or give to mother or girlfriend as gift. Not know for sure." He dangled it from its chain. "*Jou* think he died for this?"

"Not only for that one. He died because he found the temple. I'm not certain The Trawlers even knew he sent the pieces out of the country until after the fact. They simply wanted to keep the secret about the temple's location."

"Or maybe *El Chullachaqui* no want to be disturb."

"Maybe." She shifted in her chair to cut the glare from the screen. "Have you learned anything else?"

"*Si.* I show necklace to friend at museum, and he say it like a treasure map. Shows where temple is. The one my friend found."

"Like a treasure map to the treasure?"

"*Si.*"

"It doesn't lead to any other temples?"

"No, only this one."

"Well, that won't help the authorities protect any other sites. And should keep The Trawlers happy."

"And *la policia* also say they have witness to my friend falling. He

181

tell them he know nothing of secret society, but he has tattoo on hand. They know he lying. They—um—convince him to tell truth. He admit he member, followed my friend who boasted in *bar* about finding treasure. But says my friend fell. Not pushed. He tell people he saw monster. Scare them into believing *El Chullachaqui* guarding the area. To keep temple location a secret. He proud of what he does, he say."

"What do you think?"

The Peruvian shrugged. "*La policia* say all along it was an accident. Maybe is, maybe not. Maybe we never know the truth."

"I'm still sorry your friend is dead. I'm sad for you."

"Yes, we friends long time. He not know Jesus." Rogelio's frown turned to a smile. "You went to church, *sí?*"

"Yes."

"You like?"

"We did."

"You go back?"

"Yes. In fact, we went to a meeting last evening. About joining the church. And we made a decision."

His brow pulled down. "Decision?"

"Yes. I think you'd call us your new brother and sister in the Lord."

A grin filled with white teeth split his face. "Ah, such excellent news. Carmen will be so glad to hear when I tell her."

"We might ask you questions. I think we have a lot to learn."

"*Sí.* Will last for all your life. Many questions."

"Well, I won't keep you. I'm sure you want to get back to your wife."

"One more thing. *La policia* say tracks near where my friend fell resemble stories of monster, but they were made by a person with a goat heel or something carved fixed to bottom of left shoe."

"Might be the same person who left the tracks here in our town."

Rogelio's eyes widened. "I no think so. He is arrested here in Iquitos. In jail. For three days now. *La policia* say he threaten somebody else unless they pay him money."

182

"Blackmail?"

"*Sí*, blackmail."

"Somebody else is using the same method to scare us into staying quiet."

"Or else *La Chullachaqui* visit you."

Carly waited for her new friend to laugh. Chuckle. Grin. Something. Anything to bely his words. When he didn't, she said goodbye and disconnected.

Was it possible? If she believed a supernatural God could change her life, why couldn't another supernatural creature exist also?

Or was there a more rational human explanation?

She had a feeling she would soon find the answers to these questions.

+ + +

Well, that was too close for comfort. A quick getaway then drive sedately out of town. Pull off the highway onto a narrow logging lane. Pause and gather my thoughts.

The nosey accountant's husband was a surprise. Who knew the man could run so fast? A chuckle. Propelled by love and anger, perhaps? Whatever, as *los Americanos* would say.

Although what did that mean? Not exactly translatable into *Española*.

What to do next? If the accountant knew what was best for her, she'd find the other necklace and bring it to the shop as agreed. Maybe a message to remind her of the seriousness of the situation? No, she wouldn't involve *la policia*. Would she?

Chapter 19

As Mike drove to the hospital, he shook his head at his wife, seated next to him, holding the coffee cup as far away from her body as she could. "Set it in the cup holder."

Her nose wrinkled. "Really? There could be spider guts that would get on our car. No way."

"What about the guts you could be getting on your hands?"

The container wobbled, then she lowered it to her lap, gripping the container between her knees. "Better?"

"Only if you don't get distracted and lose your hold."

She glanced down at the floor. "Maybe I could put it between my feet? That way, there's nowhere for it to drop. Then the worst thing that could happen is the cup might tip over but it's dead, so it's not going anywhere. Second, it's too big to get out of that teensy-tiny hole. And thirdly. Well, there is no third. It's dead."

He snickered. "You've already thought this through in your head, haven't you?"

"Several times."

When they pulled into the hospital parking lot, the cup remained clenched between her ankles. He came around to her side of the car and opened the door. "Why don't you hand it over?"

She eyed him up and down, eyes narrowed and lips pursed. As if unsure he made a worthy spider-bearer. "I don't know. . . "

He held out a hand. "Come on. I won't drop it. Or lose it." He leaned closer. "Or eat it."

Her mouth turned down. "Don't even mention it." She tightened her hold on the cup. "I think I'd better. . ."

He exhaled. "If you don't stop that, the poor creature will be mush. Road kill."

"But Mike. . . "

He straightened, hands on hips. "Who is the one who loses their balance? Falls? Drops stuff? Is that me?" He tapped a forefinger to his temple. "Nope, not me."

"Unfair use of unidentified symptoms. Could be I'm tired. Too much caffeine. Not enough chocolate."

He accepted the cup with one hand and assisted her out with the other. "Is chocolate deficiency really a thing?"

She raised her chin. "Maybe. Why not?"

This time he laughed out loud. "In your dreams." He held his free hand out, and she slid hers in, neat as a glove. "Let's go see if Amanda is ready, then we'll take this beast to her doctor."

Thankful when they arrived at the shop owner's room without incident, he stepped aside to let her go in first—to scope out the situation, more than anything else. No point in encountering Amanda in an embarrassing situation he could never unsee.

However, she sat up in bed, lunch tray set before her. Mike's stomach rumbled. Yes, it was lunch time. Maybe he could convince Carly to check out the hospital cafeteria today.

"Ready to go?" Carly claimed the chair beside the bed. "We have a lot of news."

"Lunch just arrived." Amanda removed the lid from a short Styrofoam container about the size of two good mouthfuls. "Cream of mushroom soup." She glanced first at Carly then at Mike. "Mind if I eat while we talk? Don't want it to get cold."

Carly waggled her fingers. "Go ahead."

The younger woman dipped her spoon into the creamy concoction and sipped as though in the presence of the Queen of England, pinky in the air and all. No slurping. No tipping the container

186

back and downing it in one draught.

My table manners might scare the woman more than the big, hairy spider in Carly's cup.

He leaned against the windowsill and considered whether he should place the cup on the tray. He stifled a smile as he imagined her opening it to cream and sugar the hot beverage, screaming and dropping it when she saw its contents.

Nah, he'd best not. She might lose it in the sheets. Or on the floor. And they'd never get a positive identification.

He set the cup beside him instead, content to let his wife fill Amanda in on the goings-on at the shop today. He turned away from the conversation behind him and studied the courtyard below. Just noon, and already a full day. First, spearing the spider. Then Carly being attacked. Him chasing the strange man, who may or may not have been the intruder.

If not, some poor office worker out for fresh air and a smoke. Wow, he'll have a story to tell his wife over dinner.

Thinking about food made his tummy growl again, and he eyed the lunch tray. Did she plan to eat everything hidden in containers and under lids? Would she offer him something? Such as her half-melted sherbet? Yum. He liked soft ice cream. Or her yogurt? He turned around and checked the flavor. Never mind. He wasn't a big fan of peach.

She lifted the lid on her entrée, and his mouth watered. Salmon cakes. Whooeee.

But she seemed oblivious to his half-starved presence as she picked at the food and listened to Carly's rendition of the man who forced his way into the back room. The way his wife told the story, the man was there way longer than the few minutes she'd told him.

Or maybe that was because she was expounding on the details.

Her word for imagination.

"He was so close, I could practically see the hairs in his nose."

Amanda set her fork aside and frowned. "Really?"

Carly shook her head. "Not really. He was wearing a full ski mask."

187

"What happened then?"

"He commanded me to have the necklace there at three this afternoon. Or. Else."

"But you don't have the necklace."

Carly sat back in her chair. "No. And honestly, that concerns me."

"What are you going to do?"

"Not sure. Yet. But we thought we'd check and make sure you only received four necklaces, right?"

"Right. And you said you talked to Rogelio, and he found one in his friend's house. Which makes five." Amanda nibbled at a corner of a dinner roll then set it aside. "Except this man won't believe you when you say the other piece never left Peru."

"Probably not. But I have some ideas." Carly glanced at Mike. "But the good news is we caught the spider that bit you."

The shop owner shuddered and closed her eyes. "I don't even want to think about it." She held up her hand. "It's still red and sore. I'm lucky to be alive."

"Mike has it in that cup."

Amanda shrank away as he neared her. "I don't want to see it."

He offered what he hoped was a reassuring smile. "It's okay. Carly stabbed it with a pen."

As if on cue, his wife leaned forward. "And then I dropped the pen in the trash after I slid the spider into the cup and put the lid on."

The younger woman didn't seem convinced. "I don't know."

Mike pushed the cup closer until it was about a foot from her face. "I'll hold it, and you can peek inside."

Amanda wrapped her hands around his wrists then glared up at him. "It's not that I don't trust you. . ."

"But you don't trust me." So much for jiggling the cup when she got her eye close to the hole. "Want to hold it?"

"No."

He moved the cup a few inches and she squinted as she peered through the hole. "See anything?"

"No."

Pushing against her hands restraining his movement, he pried at the lid. "I can open it."

She squealed and pushed him away. "Please, don't."

Carly snatched the cup from him. "She's seen enough. Let me get on with my story."

He nodded and returned to the windowsill. Sometimes, girls could be so finicky.

"And if that wasn't enough excitement, then this strange guy was lurking across the street from your shop."

Amanda gasped. "The same man?"

"Don't know. Like I said, I didn't see his face in your store because of the mask."

"So, what happened?"

"Mike chased after him. But he had a car parked down by the harbor."

"Did you get a license plate?"

Mike shook his head. "None."

A nurse poked her head in through the doorway. "One more test result before we release you. Should be an hour or so."

Amanda's bottom lip jutted out. "Fine."

Carly stood. "That gives us time to deliver the spider. We'll be back."

Amanda pushed her lunch tray away, and Mike perused its shattered remains. Everything with a small nibble or a forkful eaten. Ruined for him being offered anything.

Life could be so unfair.

+ + +

Carly leaned across the cafeteria table separating her from her husband. "This was an outstanding idea. Since we couldn't see Dr. Litvin for an hour and Amanda has to wait, too, this has been like killing two birds with one stone."

He polished off the last bite of his Reuben and washed it down with a swig of soda. "I got hungry watching Amanda eat."

She grinned. "You get hungry for no good reason at all."

"Well, I had an excellent one this time." He inched his tray aside and gazed at hers. "You going to eat all those fries?"

She shook her head at him. "Guess not. And what's the reason this time?"

"It's the lunch hour. If we were home, we'd be eating now."

He jabbed his fork into three or four fries and liberated them from her plate and onto his own. After dunking them solidly into the Olympic-sized pool of ketchup, he downed them one at a time before licking his fingers and beaming at her.

She glanced around, hoping nobody noticed his child-like manners. Would the man never grow up? Then again, who were they trying to impress? Maybe she needed to lighten up. She picked up her soda and blew bubbles into the beverage, drawing another chortle from her husband at her own food-related hijinks.

She set the cup down. "I thought Amanda would jump out of that bed and run down the hall, screaming like a banshee."

"She wasn't really playing along very well, was she?"

Carly settled down. "Maybe I wouldn't either if I had to spend several days in hospital because that creature bit me."

Mike nodded. "I might have been too hard on her."

"Perhaps a mite. Then again, maybe she needed to loosen up a bit, too." Carly rolled her eyes. "Amanda always makes everything all about her."

"When do we see the doctor?" He tapped the lid of the takeout coffee cup. "I'd like to hand this off to somebody else."

"It gives me the creeps. You know me, I don't mind spraying something. Or whacking it with a shovel. But this was a little too up close and personal for my liking." She glanced at her phone. "We see him in about—" She stood and gathered their trays. "Five minutes. Let's go."

They stood outside the internist's office four and a half minutes later. Carly patted her cheeks. "Am I red in the face?"

"Nope. You are positively healthy. Ruddy. Glowing."

She groaned. Just what she needed. "Right." She drew a breath and knocked. "Dr. Litvin?"

"Come in."

She opened the door and stepped through, with Mike close on her heels, cup in hand. "Hi, We're the Turnquists. Amanda's friends."

A thin man somewhere between forty and sixty turned from a microscope on a table near the window. He stood and crossed the room. "What do we have here?"

Mike handed over the cup. "We're pretty sure it's the spider that bit Amanda."

The doctor glanced at them. "Dead?" When Mike nodded, his shoulders slumped a half-inch. "Too bad." He pried off the lid, studied the carcass a moment, then nodded. "As we thought. Brazilian Wandering Spider. Rare in these parts, as you might expect. Still, we see a dozen cases a year or so along the Eastern Seaboard. Mostly in bananas and produce from South America. Only a few survive the trip since most food is shipped in refrigerated containers. I think I've heard of one bite in the last ten years." He shook the cup. "I'd have loved to study a live specimen."

"Sorry. Maybe next time." Carly sidled closer and glanced into the cup. Ugh. Just as ugly now as when she'd last seen it, skewered on the end of an advertising pen from the diner. No doubt Victoria would be disgusted to see what her promo dollars accomplished. "How did you know how to treat her?"

"When we realized it wasn't food poisoning, we asked more questions. She saw it after the fact. Described it as best she could. Not many spiders that size around here, and once she said the package came from Peru, I did a little research on the Internet. There were still several choices, but we had an all-around anti-venom that did the trick."

"Thanks, Doc." Carly gripped Mike's hand. "Come on. We have another stop to make."

"We do?" He glanced at her as they left the office and headed for the front door. "Where?"

"Jacob Roy. I think he's holding back on me."

"You mean you haven't beaten the truth out of him yet?"

"Most of it. But there's one more piece of the puzzle that's not making any sense. Hopefully, he has it, because otherwise, I'm working on

191

a puzzle with no solution." Her cell phone rang. "Hi, Amanda. We're on our way."

"Bad news. They want me to stay a little longer."

"No worries. Let us know and we'll come and spring you."

She updated Mike, and three minutes later they pulled into the gas station and parked beside the small building that held the office, the mechanic's bay, restroom, and supply room. Jacob came out to meet them, wiping his hands in his ever-present semi-greasy rag. He leaned on the door on her side after she rolled down her window.

Carly smiled at him. Did he buy those cloths in that condition? Or was that as clean as they got? "Hi, Jacob. How's business?"

"Not bad." He glanced up and down the street. "No rush on yet. And you?"

"About the same."

"Mr. T, you shouldn't let this beautiful woman out without you being around to protect her, you know."

Mike grinned and leaned closer. His unique combination of lime-scented soap and spicy aftershave tickled her nose. And awakened her love for this man who stood beside her no matter what trouble she found herself in. "I know. But she says you keep her safe and out of trouble, so I don't worry much."

Jacob straightened. "Ayuh."

Carly glanced at the bay. "No car in for service today?"

"Nope. Like I said. No rush."

"You told me the other day you haven't rented a car lately, either."

"Not in the automobile renting business."

"Have you lent anybody one of the cars usually sitting around your lot?"

He bent over and peered at her. "Why you askin' me all these questions? Don't you believe me?"

She held his gaze, noting the tiny twitch under one eye, the way he glanced from side to side. Nervous-like. "Just trying to understand whatever is going on here in town." She laid a hand on the liver-spotted, papery hand. "You don't have to be afraid, Jacob. The sooner we figure out who is at the bottom of all this, the quicker we can catch him and get back to our lives."

He pulled his hand from her touch and his brow pulled down. "You don't know who you're messin' with, Miss Carly."

She grinned. "Come on, Jacob. You don't really believe all this nonsense about a monster, do you?"

"Danger." He spat out the single word like the syllables burned his tongue. "You can poke your nose in all you like. You can't prove what you're saying."

She opened the car door and exited, forcing the older man back a few steps. "Now you've got me wondering what you're not telling me." When Mike stood beside her, she pulled her shoulders back and stuck out her chin. "You allowed somebody to use your car. And they gave you cash for the deal. Who was it?"

"What makes you think you're right?"

"Oh, I don't know. The statement about not renting. And not being able to prove it. Which means you don't think it's a real business transaction unless it's on the books. And since it's not, there's no record." She peered at him. "Am I right?"

His shoulders slumped. "He said if I told anybody, he'd come back and visit on me a world of hurt. Or words to that effect."

She laid a hand on his forearm. "Nobody will touch a single hair on your head."

He offered her a lopsided smile. "He'd have to search awhile for one of them. I forget what they look like myself." A deep sigh. "Short, squat man. Dark skin, but not black, if you know what I mean? Not Hispanic. Or maybe he is. But he talks like an American. But not quite?"

She nodded, having noticed the same thing about the man who forced his way into the back room. "Understood. Any idea where he's staying?"

"Not in town. Comes down off the highway. But he never told me. And I didn't ask."

"When's he supposed to return the car?"

"Today. Then his mission will be done, whatever that is. And he'll

193

be leaving."

Mike sidled forward. "And when did he tell you this?"

"Couple of hours ago when he stopped for gas."

Just after he threatened her.

She thanked Jacob for his help and returned to the car. When Mike slid into the driver's seat, she pointed. "Let's go home." She pulled her cell phone from her purse. "But first I'll call Chief Donovan and let him in on the next part of the plan."

When Mike groaned, she patted his arm. "Relax. I've got this."

Another groan.

She smiled. "And I've got you to bail me out of whatever pit I dig myself into. Right?"

He nodded as he navigated up Old Tom's Hill.

He might agree, but he wasn't happy about it.

Great. He didn't even know the rest of her plan yet.

Once he did, he'd have excellent reasons not to be pleased.

+ + +

Three o'clock wouldn't come soon enough. Turn in the car and get out of town. Hopefully, at least one step ahead of the cops.

Another glass of water. Something to eat. Pack the small carry-on. Then leave about ten minutes to get back to the shop.

Boy howdy as a character said on a television show last night.

And if that nosey accountant didn't come through as promised— well, she'd get what was coming to her.

Chapter 20

Three o'clock found Carly sitting in the work area of Amanda's shop, sipping a sweet iced tea. Her hand trembled when she set the plastic cup on the desk, and she stared at her fingers. Nerves? Or perhaps this giant pink elephant in the room that neither she nor Mike wanted to talk about?

The one with MS tattooed all over it.

The wall clock over the desk showed one minute past. Maybe her anonymous visitor changed his mind and skipped town. She could only dream that was the case. Somehow, with all the time and effort he'd invested, she didn't think that particular course of action a likely one.

She glanced at the door to make certain she'd left the deadbolt unlocked. Check. By twisting to one side, she could see the front door. Not that he'd used that ingress before, but stranger things had happened. To her. To people who she knew. To strangers, no doubt.

Like Rogelio. A man she'd never meet this side of a miracle. And yet she felt she knew so much about him. And his friend. He wanted a better life. She grunted. Imagine that two hundred dollars—that's what he hoped to get for the piece—could be a life-changing amount. Hard to believe.

Yet now he lay dead because of that dream of getting ahead. No, maybe not even that—perhaps he simply wanted to catch up. And all because somebody else—The Trawlers—thought they had the better way. Keep all Peruvian artifacts not only in the country but buried deep in their vaults and their tombs and their hidden temples.

Well, what was the benefit to that course of action? Nobody could enjoy the history and the skill of the shadowy names in their country's past if they didn't know about it.

She took another sip. Somewhere—maybe on a sympathy card a long time ago—she'd read a phrase intended to give hope and comfort amid a distressing time: SO LONG AS A PERSON IS REMEMBERED, THEY STILL LIVE.

Perhaps Rogelio would remember his friend for many years to come. Would share stories of his bravery in seeking hidden Quechan temples. Would recall his love of climbing mountains, of exploring, of—

The back doorknob rattled, the door swished open, and the stranger stood before her like a ghost in the night. Daylight flooded in behind him and surrounded him, illuminating him like some kind of rock star on a stage, about to go into his trademark act. Like smashing a guitar over her head? Or biting off the head of a chicken?

She shivered. No need to be nervous. She'd done as he commanded. Be here on time. Well—a glance at the clock—he's the one three minutes late.

He growled as though reading her mind. "Wanted to be certain you were here alone."

"And?"

"You are."

"Hopefully that raises me a notch or two in your estimation of how stupid you think me."

The words seared her throat, but she uttered them anyway.

Let him think he's in control. Let him think you'll do anything he says.

She smiled. "Almost didn't recognize you without your mask." She narrowed her eyes. "Nate."

She took another long draught on her tea, watching him over the lid. "It's not here."

"I told you to bring it with you." He crossed the ten feet and grabbed her arm, shaking her like a rag doll. "Are you playing games with me?"

She slapped at his hand. "Let me go."

196

He pulled her close, his breath hot but yeasty. Stale but not sour. And something else. Mint? "Where is it?"

Nate's dark eyes bored into hers, his nose inches from hers. She struggled against his chest. Muscular. Wiry. Not an ounce of fat on him. His hands gripped her upper arms, pinching and squeezing, no doubt leaving fingerprint-shaped bruises. A gold chain glinted around his neck. She leaned closer, taking care not to breathe on him. No point in giving him any ideas. Even though she was almost old enough to be his mother.

Or his much older sister, at least.

A crucifix peeked from below his throat at the neck of his polo shirt.

Interesting. A man of both religion and crime? How did one align with the other?

Which made her think about her own life for a millisecond. Not that she was a criminal, of course. No, in fact, she was a good person, wasn't she?

He rattled her teeth with another stiff shake. "Where is it?"

"I'll take you to it."

His hands interlaced around her neck. "No tricks."

"First, I'd like to know why you're here."

He smirked. "To get back what belongs to my country."

"You already got it. The four necklaces."

He shook his head. "Not four. Five."

"One never left Peru."

His eyes widened, the near-black irises stark against the white. "Not possible."

"Yeah, seems he hid one in his house. Maybe as a gift for his mother."

"Makes no difference. He stole. He knew the consequences."

"So, your gang is well-known as enforcers? Your people know that taking artifacts out of the country is illegal?"

He practically spat and adjusted his hold. "Not just illegal. Immoral. Punishable by death."

"Is that why you killed him?"

197

His mouth turned down. "I didn't kill him. That was *El Chullachaqui*. As our traditions say. He is the guardian of everything Peruvian."

She frowned. "Please. Everybody knows that's a fairy tale to scare children from wandering into the jungle alone."

"No. Is real. I saw it once."

Likely story.

"And Victor?"

He tilted his head to one side. "Who?"

"The delivery driver."

"Oh, *si*. Looking for what is my country's."

"You assaulted him, kidnapped him, and left him?"

"Yes. But I knew he would be found quickly."

"The spider?"

He grinned. "Yes. Devious, no?" He shook her again. "And before we drag this out until the sun goes down, yes, I broke into this little shop. And into that woman's house. And into the police station."

"Are you the one lurking around town? Peeking in windows?"

He exhaled. "Yes, and I struck you when you surprised me in your garden. I didn't plan that." His shoulder slumped a millimeter. "Sorry."

"I don't believe you."

"What? That I'm sorry?"

"No. About not killing that man in Peru. The police are fairly certain the tracks were made by somebody wearing a boot on one foot and a peg-leg with a goat hoof on the other."

He sniggered. "You can't prove I killed him. Or left the tracks."

"Well, you left the tracks in the alley. And in the park."

He nodded. "Couldn't help myself. That old man was so sure he'd seen something supernatural." He yanked her toward him. "Are you done asking questions?"

She nodded, a scream stuck in her throat.

He tightened his grip, and white lights danced around the periphery of her vision. She pried at his fingers as the white turned to black.

She couldn't breathe.

He was killing her.

This made little sense.

And it absolutely wasn't the way she envisioned this going.

When he didn't release her, she used her last rational thought to kick him in the shin.

Thankfully, it worked.

He released her—well, actually, he relaxed his grip on her throat, long enough so she could draw in a half-breath. And just in time, too. She tried another tactic.

She slumped to the floor, forcing him to choose between letting her go or collapsing with her under the momentum of her middle-age well-padded body.

He chose wisely and let her go.

Which meant she thunked down harder than she'd planned, banging her elbow on the desk as she went. Wow. A direct hit to the funny bone wasn't even a little humorous. No pun intended.

But her move accomplished the desired effect.

Nate leaned over her and grabbed her by the shoulders of her shirt. "Get up."

Instead of complying, she kicked at his knee, knocking him off balance. "Get off me."

He growled, and she wrapped her arms around her head and closed her eyes.

A scuffle. A grunt. A click.

She opened her eyes.

Mike peered down at her, his forehead creased and the wrinkles around his eyes deep. Nate slumped over the desk, hands behind his back, cuffs pinning them in place. And Chief Donovan patted the man down.

Carly sat up, rubbing her elbow. "What took you guys so long?"

The chief straightened. "No weapons." He turned Nate around to face them. "We had to wait until he admitted to something we could charge him with. Murder would have been better, although that would have meant extradition. Kidnapping is almost as good."

199

Nate wrestled against his bonds. "I didn't kill him."

Donovan clamped a ham-sized fist on the Peruvian's shoulder. "Settle down there. We've got enough charges on you to make certain you won't be loose for many years to come." He spun the criminal around and handed him off to Officer Meyers. "Don't let your guard down for a minute. This one's slippery, I think."

Nate twisted around and glared at Carly where she stood beside Mike. "This is not the end. You will regret this. And very soon."

A shiver ran down her spine at his words. She'd been threatened by the very best over the years, but this man—well, he was more intense than any of the others.

He really scared her, because he really believed what he said.

+ + +

When Doc Walsh delivered his verdict at five minutes past four, Carly almost laughed.

He said she had a cute something-or-other.

Mike squeezed her hand. "Could you tell us that again?"

Doctor Walsh grinned. "Quite the mouthful, isn't it?" He glanced at her medical chart which lay on the desk before him. "Acute Disseminated Encephalomyelitis. Medical folk find it a tongue tangler, too, so we call it ADEM."

Carly drew a breath and let it out in a rush. "Will it kill me?"

"Unlikely."

"And what is it?"

"An inflammation of the brain, in your case." He pulled a plastic cast of a head toward him and opened it at the hinge. Using his pen, he pointed to various parts of the brain and explained their purpose before setting the model aside. "What sets ADEM apart from other illnesses and diseases, such as encephalitis, is that the myelin is damaged. And this interferes with how your brain works. Can affect stability, vertigo, vision, thinking, for example."

Mike nodded. "And you're sure it isn't MS?"

"Absolutely. The MRI confirmed there are no old or new lesions on the brain, which would signal a positive diagnosis of MS."

Mike stood. "Good. Well, thanks for your help. Sorry to take your time." He smiled down at her. "Let's go."

Doc Walsh held up a hand. "Wait a minute. It's not MS, but you will need to make some changes." He waited until Mike resumed his seat before continuing. "We'll want you to come in each day for an intravenous corticosteroid treatment to combat the inflammation. You'll see immediate improvement in a few days, with expected complete recovery within six to twelve months."

She smiled. "Well, this all sounds like it will soon be behind me."

He shook his head. "We saw areas of damage where the sheath of your brain impinged on areas associated with left-body motor skills. Also, a bruise-like area in your frontal lobe, which initiates and coordinates higher cognitive skills."

Her smile dropped away. "So, that means?"

"You could experience ongoing memory issues, critical thinking problems, weakness in your hands and feet that could cause you to drop things or trip easily. We won't know for sure at this point. But I would suggest you dial your work back. I'd prefer that you not drive, but if you insist, make it a brief trip, like here in town. Avoid stress."

At this, Mike snorted, and she tugged on his hand and frowned at him. "Hush." She turned to the doctor. "Sounds like life as I knew it is over."

"Not immediately. And not completely. But drastically curtailed. Still, there are other activities you can adopt, such as reading, puzzles, walking, travel, scrapbooking."

She rolled her eyes. Scrapbooking.

Maybe she could go to the jail and ask Nate to kill her now.

+ + +

At home, after supper, Carly lingered at the table with a second cup of decaf. Mike cleared the dishes—she'd cooked—so she kept him company while he slaved over a hot sinkful of pots and pans.

Well, two pans, really, and a baking dish, but who was counting?

She spied the new Bible the pastor gifted them with on Monday evening and pulled it toward her. Inside the cover, the pamphlet entitled

WHEN IS GOOD, GOOD ENOUGH? Her notes covered every page.

She smiled and tapped the paper. "You know, this afternoon, before Nate tried to strangle me, I had a moment of lucidity when I compared myself to him. I mean, he's a criminal, right? Wearing a cross. How does that jive?"

Mike turned and leaned against the counter. "We hear of supposedly religious people doing hurtful things. A pastor who has an affair. A church secretary who embezzles. A priest who—"

She held up a hand to stop him. "Okay. I get the idea."

He sat across from her. "Pastor Wilkes said God doesn't grade on a curve. That wrong is wrong. Sin is sin. It's all the same."

She jutted out her bottom lip. "But surely some things must be worse than others. A cop killer is worse than somebody who shoots a clerk in a convenience store robbery, right?"

He smiled. "Unless that clerk is you. Then what?"

She sat back and folded her arms over her chest. "Point taken. What about child molesters? *They* are the scum of the earth."

Mike tapped the Bible. "According to a verse Pastor Wilkes mentioned in church on Sunday, *we* are said scum. Every single one of us."

She exhaled. "Which means me thinking I'm better than Nate because I'm not a criminal is wrong?"

"Right." He scooted his chair around the corner of the table until he sat beside her. Then he reached out and looped an arm over her shoulder. "Same for me. What are we going to do about it?"

She turned to the last page of the pamphlet—correction, tract, as Pastor Wilkes called it—and pointed. "There's a list here. NEXT STEPS, it's called." She ran a finger down the words. "We found a church, have a Bible, and we've asked God for forgiveness." She stopped at the next item. "Find a mentor."

Mike nodded and pulled her close. "I know the exact couple. Larry and Yvonne."

"He gave you the pocket testament, right?"

"He did. And that got us started."

202

She smiled. "Sounds like God was already on the move."

+ + +

Never one to leave a thing undone, Carly slipped into her chair at her desk and turned on her computer. Mike followed her. In fact, he hadn't let her out of his sight all evening.

Hopefully this was a phase and not her new norm.

She opened her email program and scanned its contents. Ah, one from Rogelio. She read the first paragraph then gasped. "Mike, you've got to listen to this."

He leaned across his desk. "What is it?"

"An email. From Rogelio. He said he talked to the police today in Iquitos about his friend's case, and they've closed it, convinced they have the murderer."

"We already knew that."

"Right. But there's more. The man they arrested said he didn't leave fake tracks."

Mike sat back. "It's what he says."

"Well, he's still in custody, so he couldn't have made these new tracks."

"What new tracks?"

"The ones they found at the place where a little boy wandered off from his family and was gone for hours. They went searching for him but couldn't find him. Finally, they called in the police, who alerted a search and rescue team."

"Did they find him?"

"Yes. Safe and sound. Jabbering on about a little man who pulled him up from a cliff he'd slipped over. Apparently same little man took him to his cave, gave him something to eat and drink, and returned him to within two hundred feet of the search team. Safe and sound."

"What's so strange about that? I'm sure there are lots of folks everywhere who'd help a lost child."

She continued reading. "The boy said the little man was the same size as the boy's two-year-old sister. And he simply disappeared."

"Sounds like childhood imagination. The kid didn't want to get in

203

trouble for not listening to the adults."

"But here's the best part." She checked to make certain she had his attention. She did. "They found tracks at the cliff edge where the child almost went over that led to a cave where there'd been a recent campfire, then back to where the search party found him. A booted and a goat track led up to the edge, turned into two bare feet, then another pair of smaller feet alongside. To the cave and in the cave. Then away from the cave to where the boy was left. Then the larger bare feet stopped and turned into the odd feet again before fading away just inside the jungle boundary."

"Not possible."

"That's what the police thought. They took dogs to follow the trails. Total confusion. They scented on the boy's tracks, but it was like the barefoot footprints and the odd tracks didn't exist, even though they took plaster casts of the lot." She exhaled. "What do you think of that?"

"Somebody trying to perpetuate the legend?"

She grinned. "Sounds like *El Chullachaqui* doesn't need any help. He gets about just fine on his own."

+ + +

Later that evening, Mike stepped out of the shower and dried off, enjoying the luxurious Egyptian cotton bath towel that felt like an exfoliator. Sure, he knew what that was. He paid attention when Carly talked about such things.

Speaking of which, she'd been much too quiet all evening. Whenever he pressed her, she said she was fine, but he knew different.

And speaking of which, she was too quiet now.

He peeked into the bedroom. She sat at the dressing table, hairbrush in hand, gazing into the mirror. "You okay?"

Her tiny jump indicated she'd been miles away, deep in thought. "Uh-huh."

He wrapped the towel around his waist and padded over to the bed. "What's on your mind?"

She set the brush aside and toyed with her hair, flipping her bangs first one way then the other. Finally, she paused, resting her hands in her lap. "Nothing. Well, lots of things, I guess. We've had a full day."

He chuckled. "A typical day." Then he remembered the doctor's office. "Well, not so ordinary, I guess. You stabbing a venomous spider. Prying information from poor old Jacob. Almost getting throttled by a criminal. Getting said criminal to spill the works. All of that is a run-of-the-mill day for you."

She rose and sat beside him, laying her head on his shoulder. "But the rest isn't."

"Nope. You're right about that. It's a lot to process."

She twined her fingers into knots. "I feel like I'm losing a part of me. If I can't work—and it sounds like I shouldn't—then what will I do?"

He planted a kiss on the top of her head. "What would you like to do?"

"I don't know. I've only ever wanted to work with numbers." She peered up at him, her eyes bright with unshed tears. "I don't want to be a burden. To you or the kids."

"Don't think like that. I've decided that since you're retiring, I'll do the same." He laid a finger across her mouth when she objected. "We've talked about this before. We have a solid investment portfolio, plenty in our retirement accounts. We've put in our years, and now it's time to enjoy our relatively good health and make the most of the time we have." He closed his eyes. What would he do now that he didn't have to write computer programs? He opened his eyes. "You know, I've always wanted to take a shop course at the community college but never had the time. I've read a lot about these hydrogen/electric hybrid cars. I think there's a grand future in them."

She straightened. "You would?"

"Uh-huh. I could retrofit cars with the parts needed to convert them." He stood and peeked out the window. "I could convert that shed near the back fence into a workshop. Build a cover over there for rainy days. And—" He turned when she chuckled. "Don't mock me. I know I can do it."

"Oh, I know you can, too." She crossed the room and stood beside him, her arm looped through his. "I've solved so many mysteries, I think I could fill a bookshop with my adventures. I want to take a creative writing class so I can write mystery books. Maybe we could go back to school together."

He pulled her close and kissed her tenderly on the mouth. She pressed against him, and his plans for the future flew from his mind. Another kiss, this one deeper, and she took him by the hand and led him toward the bed.

When he bent to kiss this woman again, the one he hoped to grow old with, she wriggled out of his grasp and giggled.

He cuddled her close to his side. "What's so funny?"

"We are facing all these life changes, but one thing will never change."

He turned over to face her. "What's that?"

"I'll still be a full-time job for you."

"Come here." When she scootched over, he pressed his lips to her ear. "For which I will always be grateful."

She turned off the light, and the darkness enveloped them—and their love for each other—like a warm, fuzzy blanket.

He sat up. "Wait a minute. Fill a bookshop with your adventures? Which ones don't I know about?"

BUT WAIT. . . THERE'S MORE. . .

THANKS SO MUCH for sticking with Carly—and with me—until the end.

Yes, this is the finale book in the By the Numbers series.

If you enjoyed this story, I hope you'll leave a review online at Amazon, Smashwords, and wherever else you usually leave reviews. And if you haven't read the first books in the series, no worries. You can read them in order, or in any order you choose. You can even save money on the print copies and purchase them in the form of the Omnibus Collection, Volumes 1, 2, 3, and very soon, 4 – three complete novels in each volume.

So what's up next for Carly, besides retirement?

If you really want to know, watch for *Mysterious Ink*, a segue novella between this series and the next, which fast-forwards us to 2020. Join Carly and her granddaughter Margie as they work together to solve another mystery, which launches Margie into her own series. The first will release in December 2020, then every six months until Margie tells me she is done.

You can follow me at www.LeeannBetts.com or
www.AllBettsAreOff.wordpress.com
I'm active on Facebook and Twitter.

If you aren't already subscribed to my quarterly newsletter, hop on over to my website and fill out the form.

Acknowledgements

First and foremost, to the one True God, His Son Jesus Christ, and the Holy Spirit.
Without them, no story would be worth telling

To my husband Patrick. My biggest fan.

To my special, real-life friends in Peru, Carmen and Rogelio. Just like the characters in this book, they are honest, God-fearing people. Apart from that, my characters bear no other resemblance to my dear friends.

To my other special, real-life friends, Larry and Yvonne. Because of them, we're proud to serve in The Gideons International, a Christian organization best known for placing Bibles in hotels. However, our chief mission is to win the lost to Christ. The Gideons International has been around for more than 120 years, and continues their ministry in more than 200 countries. If you'd like more information about how to support in prayer, financially, or through membership, check them out at:
https://www.gideons.org/

About the Author

Leeann Betts writes contemporary romantic suspense, while her real-life persona, Donna Schlachter, pens historical romantic suspense. *Risk Management* is the 12th and final story in her cozy mystery series, "By the Numbers". Watch for a segue novella in September that weaves Carly's story with the upcoming new cozy mystery series, "Mysterious Ink Bookstore Mysteries", with its first title releasing in December 2020. Together she and Donna have published more than 30 novellas and full-length novels. They ghostwrite, judge writing contests, edit, facilitate a critique group, and are members of American Christian Fiction Writers, Writers on the Rock, Christian Authors Network, Pikes Peak Writers, and Sisters in Crime. Leeann travels extensively to research her stories, and is proud to be represented by Terrie Wolf of AKA Literary LLC.

www.LeeannBetts.com Stay connected so you learn about new releases, preorders, and presales, as well as check out featured authors, book reviews, and a little corner of peace. Plus: Receive a free ebook simply for signing up for our free newsletter!

Bonanza Books-in-a-Flash: order autographed print copies of books that are shipped directly from the author.

Blog: www.AllBettsAreOff.wordpress.com

Facebook: http://bit.ly/1pQSOqV

Twitter: http://bit.ly/1qmqvB6

Books: Amazon http://amzn.to/2dHfgCE and Smashwords: http://bit.ly/2z5ecP8

What Can Be Online University: online courses on the craft of writing

Etsy online shop of original artwork, book folding art, and gift items